COME AND BE KILLED

Prescribed a holiday out of London to recover from nervous exhaustion, Florence Brown is betrayed and furious when her sister refuses to accompany her. An unsuccessful attempt to take her own life sees her dispatched to a grim nursing-home. Mid-way through her escape from the place, she encounters the genial Mrs. Jolly, who invites Florence to stay with her as a paying guest. But her new friend is not all she seems, and Florence is in deadly danger . . .

Books by Shelley Smith
in the Linford Mystery Library:

THE LORD HAVE MERCY

SHELLEY SMITH

COME AND BE KILLED

Complete and Unabridged

LINFORD
Leicester

First published in Great Britain

First Linford Edition
published 2017

A catalogue record for this book is available
from the British Library.

ISBN 978–1–4448–3348–5

Published by
F. A. Thorpe (Publishing)
Anstey, Leicestershire

Set by Words & Graphics Ltd.
Anstey, Leicestershire
Printed and bound in Great Britain by
T. J. International Ltd., Padstow, Cornwall

This book is printed on acid-free paper

PART ONE

CHILD'S PLAY

1

The Quarrel

'I'd almost given you up! You're late!' exclaimed Phoebe, as she opened the door.

The undersized little woman in the hall said nastily, 'Thanks, then I'll go,' and turned away deliberately.

Her sister caught her by the arm. 'Don't be absurd! Come in, for goodness' sake, now you're here.' She led the way into a large room, full of light and soft clear colours with flowing lines: the central apartment of her small service flat.

'Good God!' cried the other violently. 'Whatever have you done to yourself?'

'Nothing ... Oh, my hair, do you mean?' She ran a slim hand over her curls, the incredible colour now of the flaming Virginia creeper. 'I did it for the show. I never feel happy in a wig. It's

3

come out a bit bright, I admit . . . Have you had tea yet?'

Florence ignored the question and said sharply:

'You look perfectly terrible. Still, it's none of my business, if you're not ashamed . . . Well, here I am, anyway. I didn't want to come . . . Fagging myself out for nothing. Why should I? But I thought you might be interested to hear what the specialist said, that's all.'

'Well, naturally I'm interested. You always act as though I were some kind of a monster. And I asked you to come in here, because, after all, it is on your way home, isn't it?' Phoebe's voice was soothing. 'I only meant that I'd have to be starting for the theatre soon. But not yet, not yet,' she added hurriedly. 'Don't look like that. And you haven't told me whether you've had tea yet?'

'I haven't had tea; but I don't want any, so you needn't trouble yourself.' Florence jerked off her gloves, rolled them into a ball and threw them viciously on to the divan. 'I nearly fainted in Baker Street,' she remarked in a stifled, sub-acid voice.

Phoebe suppressed a sigh.

'I'm so sorry, darling. I wish you'd sit down and rest yourself, instead of fidgeting up and down. Are you sure you wouldn't like a cup of tea? It won't take a minute to make you one.'

'Oh, make it if you like. Do it if you want to — and don't if you don't. I've told you a million times, I can't be burdened with decisions,' Florence said pathetically. 'Can't you understand? If I have to decide anything it makes me feel as if the top of my head would — ' Her voice broke, and she turned away, lurching up and down the room with hunched shoulders, clasping and unclasping her hands in a furious effort to regain self-control.

Phoebe slipped quietly into the kitchenette and plugged in the electric kettle. A frown puckered the white skin between her eyebrows. What on earth was to be done with Florence?

Florence continued, speaking drily and deliberately, as though there had been no break:

'It feels as though the top of my head

would fly off, do you see? It's unbearable! I don't mean to be ratty, but it's unbearable. I don't know how I go on. Sometimes I think I'll go mad. It's awful!'

'It must be,' agreed her sister sympathetically. 'And what did the doctor say? You haven't told me yet. Take off your coat now and sit down, while I put some tea in the pot.' In moments of warmth the brogue always flattered her soft voice, actress that she was.

'I'm dog-tired,' admitted Florence, flinging off her outer clothes.

'Well,' said Phoebe, handing her a cup of hot sweet tea, 'let's hear the worst of it.' While she lit a cigarette she glanced again at the little woman crouched on the edge of the divan, her tiny thin paws clutching the warmth of the cup, for all the world like a poor little desolate monkey. 'Did you like him? Was he kind?'

'The doctor? He was as decent as they can be, I suppose,' she said grudgingly. 'You know what I think of that lot — charlatans! I daresay he was as honest as most. He certainly was thorough, I'll say that for him; asked me a million questions

— most of which I couldn't answer.' She laughed, shortly.

'And the verdict?' Phoebe glanced surreptitiously at her wristwatch.

Florence gulped down some tea before answering wryly: 'What would you imagine? Complete rest . . . from from anxiety . . . nourishing food . . . and a nice glass of port wine after meals — I don't think!' she added sarcastically.

'I don't see why you say that. Surely Hoggers will give you a break after all these years? He must know you're ill.'

'Maybe.' She put down her cup with a bang and stood up. 'The doctor says I ought to leave Hoggers,' she jerked out abruptly.

'Leave Hoggers!' Phoebe did not attempt to hide her amazement. 'After twenty years!'

'That's the idea. According to this specialist, half the trouble is that I've had twenty years of monotonous grind at the same deadly dull thing, without a break, except for a fortnight once a year. He said it's enough to send anyone potty.'

'But, leave Hoggers! *That* sounds

7

absolutely insane to me, if you like. What about your pension, may I ask?' Phoebe sat up indignantly, her bright hair curling about her shoulders.

'Exactly. He saw the difficulty — after I showed it to him. He couldn't advise me, of course; that was not his job. He merely wished to explain the facts to me: it would be wise of me — in fact, it was my duty to myself — to get another job.'

'Well, you'd be very silly to, in my opinion,' said Phoebe firmly. 'He ought to have realised that a woman in your position can't afford to throw away a decent job with a pension at the end of it.'

'Quite, quite. On the other hand, it was his duty to tell me what he believed to be at the bottom of my illness. He says I must get away, right out of London, immediately. If I don't — well! I've got a letter here that he's written to my doctor, old Paget; telling him all about it, I suppose. I ought to have at least six months, he says. They'll be furious at the works when they hear that. It couldn't be at a worse time; we're frantically busy. Still, I've promised only to take this month that they've already granted for now, and the rest later in the year.'

'You certainly ought to have a holiday — he's right there. I'm glad he's persuaded you . . . Where are you going?'

Florence walked slowly across the room.

'That's really why I came, Phee. I know in my heart that he's right and that I ought to get away for a bit, even though the thought of it scares me stiff. But — but — ' She glanced at her sister hurriedly from the corner of her eye. ' — ill as I am now, I can't face going anywhere alone. I'm too . . . I'm afraid . . . I thought . . . I hoped you'd come with me,' she ended timidly.

'You mean now, right away?' Phoebe said miserably: 'Darling! God knows I hate to refuse you, but I can't.'

Silence. Florence stood motionless with her back to Phoebe.

'I do wish I could,' Phoebe reiterated. 'I feel a wretch letting you down. Isn't there possibly anyone else you could go with?' she said, knowing the question was hopeless before she asked it. 'What can I do?' she mused, half-aloud. 'If I find someone nice for you to go with, someone reliable and kind — '

'A keeper, I suppose,' snapped Florence.

'Don't be absurd! I might come across someone decent — you never know. If I do, would you go with them?'

'A stranger! Phoebe, can't you understand? It's partly because I'm so terrified of people that I'm afraid to go away. I sweat with fear among strangers. I don't want to have to make conversation. I'm ill. I want to be looked after,' she cried appealingly.

'Yes, yes, of course,' muttered her sister. 'But what can I do?'

'Why can't you come with me?'

'But, darling, don't be unreasonable. How can I? In the middle of rehearsals of a new play! The first night is a week today.'

'They could get someone else to take your place. It's not such a very important part, after all.'

'Darling!' She had no voice left with which to express her shocked amazement.

'You don't know what you're saying!'

'I do. Very well. I'm asking you to do me a favour — make a sacrifice, if you prefer big words — and give up a rather mouldy part in some puffing modern play that probably won't run a week — '

'Thanks.'

'Come away with me! I'll pay your expenses. There! You won't lose by it at all. You could do with a change too, couldn't you? It's only for a month, Phee. You could explain to them at the theatre how it was and I expect they'd get a fill-in, some temporary understudy to take your part for just those few weeks. They would understand, Phee, I'm sure.'

Phoebe folded her sister's cold claw between her warm shapely hands.

'Florrie, old girl, it's you who don't understand. You just can't do things like that in the theatre; it isn't done. Once you get a name for unreliability, you're as good as done for.'

'I don't see how you can get a reputation for unreliability from just backing out once, in order to look after your only relative. I don't see what better reason you could have.'

'Do be sensible. You think I'm being horribly selfish, I know. But try to think of it from my angle for a minute, if you can. I don't know why you say it's a mouldy part and a rotten play when you don't know anything about it. As it happens, it's a part in a million. You know, Florrie, that there's only one thing in my life now that means anything to me — and that's my career. And now you're asking — '

'Your career! I guessed you'd bring *that* up. My God! I don't wonder Fred left you; your damn vanity always stuck in his throat. A woman of your age always wanting to exhibit herself on the stage. You should be ashamed. Dressing up and showing off! I'm nearly forty, and you're older than I am. It's disgusting!'

'There have got to be some elderly people on the stage,' said Phoebe mildly, 'or what would happen to all the 'mother' parts? That is, if you hanker after realism.'

'Oh, for the Lord's sake, spare us a monologue!' she spat out. 'I know you begin where Bernhardt and Duse left off; I've heard it all before. All right. You stick to the theatre. And I hope it'll be a comfort to you when you're in trouble . . . Where's my hat? What have you done with it?' she cried bitterly, tossing the cushions out of the chairs in her search, while blinding tears ran off her face.

'Look, darling,' said Phoebe, coming to her and putting her arms round her tenderly, 'why don't you postpone your holiday for a while? Just till we've time to look around. Why must you be off in this desperate rush?'

She shrugged away. 'Oh, what's the use of talking about it,' she snivelled. 'Leave me alone . . . I tell you I *have* to go now because my leave has already started, and because the doctor says only complete rest and freedom from all anxiety can save me now. Do you understand that? 'Can *save* me'!'

'You ought to get a grip on yourself, Florrie. It's not a bit of use going to pieces over nothing like that. You expect other people to live your life for you, and it can't be done, old girl.'

'I wouldn't expect you to show any decent feelings for me; you never have.

Will you give me my hat and let me go?'

'I'm not keeping you. I have to go now myself, or I'll be late.'

'God forbid!' snarled Florence, wiping the hot tears from her cheeks with the back of her hand.

'You're not being very easy about this, you know. You're putting the entire onus onto me, but it really isn't my fault that I'm not free just now.'

'Well, I don't think you're being very helpful either, so there you are . . . No, don't touch me. Leave me alone! I can manage to put on my coat, since I always have; and it might make you late for your precious rehearsal.'

Phoebe shrugged and went into the small compartment off the main room, called by the estate agents a bedroom. While she hunted for her outdoor clothes, she saw with irritation that she was already late. And to no purpose, what was more, for Florence was annoyed with her and nothing was settled. She would have to see what could be done about the matter . . . but not now, now she must get down to the theatre. The mirror reflected the pale curves of her oval face, the dark flower of her mouth, her hair looped in a veil. She would think of some decent place that would suit Florence and then she would take her down, see her comfortably settled in, and come back the same day. That would be best. Cheered by this reflection, she returned to her sister, who was staring gloomily out of the window munching her fingertip.

'Don't worry, Flo,' said Phoebe, struggling into her coat. 'I've got a notion up my sleeve that it will turn out all right. Leave it to me.'

'Don't put yourself out on my account,' remarked the small figure at the window. 'I'm not worth bothering about. I'm only a human being. You get on with your play-acting.'

'Now, don't be silly. And don't sulk,' she admonished kindly, turning to the glass to adjust her hat. 'Hello!' she exclaimed. 'Whoever turned the mirror with its face to the wall? What an extraordinary thing! Did you, Flo?'

At first there was no response. And then a reluctant; 'Yes.'

Phoebe stared curiously at the drooping back silhouetted against the pane.

'Why?'

'Felt like it.' She shrugged. 'Why not, for that matter?'

Phoebe laughed nervously. 'You really are barmy.'

'That's right. Rub it in. Keep on telling me I'm crazy — I'll believe it soon, and then you'll be able to have me shut up and I'll be no more trouble to anyone.'

'Don't be — '

'Do you think I don't know I'm crackers?' Florence whirled round stormily, her narrow face livid. 'I know what you think, and I know what everybody else thinks. That specialist I saw today as good as told me . . . You wanted to know why I turned that mirror round? Because I'm afraid to see my own face.'

Phoebe caught her up in her arms and murmured soothingly.

'If you only knew how tired I am!'

'Yes, yes. Poor little thing!'

'If you knew what it was like, day in, day out . . . I wish I was dead.'

'Don't say that, darling, it's unlucky.

You're depressed just now. But when we've fixed you up somewhere for a nice holiday, you'll feel quite different, and all this will seem like an ugly dream.' Phoebe controlled her impatience marvellously, ignoring the relentless ticking of the clock.

'Will you come with me, Phee?' said the small voice.

'I can't promise that, you know. But I'll see that you're all right. Don't fret about it anymore, there's a good girl. I must go now, or there'll be a deadly row; I'm terribly late already. Ring me up tomorrow morning. Or, better still, I'll ring you, just as soon as I've fixed something up. Do you fancy anywhere in particular? Margate's awfully bracing. Or would it be too cold this time of year?' she asked, drawing on her gloves as she spoke.

Florence drew away from her, buttoned up tightly within herself once more.

'Oh, for God's sake don't fix anything for me — thanks all the same. I prefer to make my own arrangements.'

Somewhat taken aback, Phoebe said equably: 'Just as you please. I thought you didn't feel up to making decisions and plans.'

'I asked you to come with me, as a guest, as a friend, as a sister. You refused. Doubtless you had very good reasons: they don't concern me. The point is, you preferred not to come. That being so, you needn't bother with me at all. I'm sorry I've taken up so much of your time and made you late, for nothing . . . See you sometime,' she said with bitter carelessness, marching to the door.

'Don't be so hasty, Flo. Why quarrel with your only sister, you foolish girl?' urged Phoebe, hurrying after her.

'Too late now . . . ' drifted back to her. 'I shall go where I choose — when I choose — and if I don't choose — I shan't.'

2

Death for a Shilling

Florence Brown had no recollection afterwards of how she reached 'home', her furnished bed-sitting-room in Arkwright Road. She had lived there for five years. It was not particularly comfortable or homey, but on the other hand it was convenient in many ways: near the Heath for a nice walk Sunday mornings or on hot summer evenings; close to a respectable shopping district; and the landlady was not unamiable as landladies go, provided one kept to the rules. Besides, the house itself was rather select, and catered specially for 'business ladies' — but was not a hostel. Florence was used to it and didn't think herself so badly off. Having reached this haven, she now flung herself on the covered divan and waited for the tumult within to subside.

She lay there, meagre and crumpled as

a scarf, and thought with despair of tomorrow. When next she became aware of her surroundings, it was dark and her room was streaked with long yellow beams from the street lamp at the corner. Whether she had been asleep, unconscious or in a trance she did not know, but she felt wretched; her head ached and all her bones were stiff with cold. If she had not been on the ground floor, she vowed she would have jumped out of the window, so abysmal was the depth of her depression. What did it matter whether she lived or died? Who would care? Not a soul on God's earth! It would be better to cut her throat right now and be done with it.

But supposing death wasn't the end? Suppose when you'd done it you found you were still alive — sort of? What then? Well, you couldn't be much worse off, could you? All that stuff about hell, nobody believed that nowadays, not even kids. God must see how hopeless it all was. Perhaps He meant her to chuck in her hand. If He didn't mean her to — seeing her suffer like this — why didn't

He do something about it? That was reasonable, wasn't it? That was a fair test. God, if He existed, was to prove His existence by coming to her aid positively, before she was able to kill herself. There!

Slightly comforted by this unreasonable wager, she rose, switched on the light and began searching for a likely weapon with which to commit suicide, subconsciously consoled by her assurance of a miraculous last-minute reprieve from God. Gas, now, there was always gas. If you lay down with your face close to the gas fire, and perhaps had a heavy cloth draped carefully over the top of the stove and enclosing your head, surely that would be effective . . . provided one had enough money in the meter, of course. How many shillings, she wondered, did it take to kill a person, a small person?

Trembling a little, she emptied the contents of her purse on to the table and spread them out — scoured among the tickets and hairpins at the bottom of the bag. She gave a foolish little laugh of relief. How like her! Not a shilling anywhere. It looked as though she couldn't kill herself if she tried . . . As if she wasn't *meant* to. Still, she mustn't leave a stone unturned that would be cheating. If her landlady was in . . .

She discovered the landlady in her brightly-lit cosy basement-parlour, knitting. She was actually a caretaker, not the landlady, but she collected the rents for her employer. Mrs. Bowles, her name was; but, although she had two grown daughters, 'Mrs.' was really a courtesy title, and the effort of turning to and bringing up two great girls single-handed had considerably soured her fundamental good nature. She raised her head with its rigid, metallic, grooved hair, to call, 'Come in!' to Miss Brown's knock.

'Good evening, Mrs. Bowles,' said Florence shyly, holding the door ajar. 'I'm so sorry to disturb you.'

'That's all right, Miss.'

'I wondered if you could let me have a few shillings — for the gas, you know. So careless of me . . . '

'Well, I'll see now. But I don't believe — ' She fetched her shabby black leather bag and busied herself inside it.

'Here, I've got three shillings. Will that do you?'

'Three shillings? I expect so. It'll have to, won't it?'

Mrs. Bowles looked at her grudgingly: 'You haven't forgotten you owe me a bob from the other night, have you?'

Florence was suddenly cold and sober as a stone, weary and ashamed.

'No, of course I haven't forgotten,' she lied. 'That's four shillings altogether. I must pay you back. I won't forget, I promise.'

'Oh, it's not keeping me awake at night. I know you're not going to run away.'

'No . . . Well, thank you, Mrs. Bowles. Good night.' She closed the door softly behind her.

Back in her room, Florence scrawled *I owe Mrs. Bowles four shillings* on a scrap of paper and left it on the imitation oak table in a prominent position. There was something so pathetic about this last testament that it brought tears to her eyes. Sniffing slightly, she dropped the coins in the meter and turned the knob. She fetched a rug and pillows from the bed and spread them neatly on the floor as close to the stove as possible. It really looked quite comfortable. She pulled back the curtains and shut the window, stuffing paper along the cracks as she had seen someone do in a film. Then she did the same beneath the door, and turned the key in the lock.

She lay down on the floor and draped the rug across the stove so that it fell in folds over her head. It was warm, rather stuffy, not unpleasant. With one finger she pushed the tap round till she heard a faint, dreary hissing.

★   ★   ★

Not long afterwards, Phoebe, home once more from the theatre, paused in the act of creaming her face, repenting of her previous impatience, and decided to ring up her sister before she went to bed, to make it up and reassure herself that Florence was all right.

There was only one 'phone in the Arkwright Road house, and that was in a passage in the basement, just outside

Mrs. Bowles' kitchen. To answer the 'phone and take messages was one of Mrs. Bowles' little jobs.

Now, Mrs. Bowles toiled upstairs to the ground floor, knocked at Miss Brown's door, called . . . knocked again more vigorously . . . rattled the handle . . . noticed the ragged edges of newspaper poking under the door. Funny, thought Mrs. Bowles, knowing she never locked herself in at night in case of fire. Going downstairs again, she informed the telephone that she could get no answer from Miss Brown . . .

'I expect she's asleep, then,' said the voice at the other end. 'Don't bother. You might tell her I rang up — it's her sister, Mrs. Moore — and ask her to give me a ring tomorrow . . . 'Bye.'

Mrs. Bowles felt an unaccustomed thumping against her ribs as she ran out into the area and looked up.

'There! She's not drawn her curtains, nor got the light on,' she muttered, and flew up the area steps, leaning as far over the railing as she dared, to peer through the dark secretive pane.

From where she stood she could see the divan was unoccupied and was still in its cheap, rather garish, modern cover. The obliging rays of the street lamp illumined an ominous dark heap by the fireplace that confirmed Mrs. Bowles' misgivings. She was not one to lose her head in a crisis, and in next to no time she had propped the window-cleaner's ladder against the wall and was standing halfway up it. She wrapped her fist in her skirt and thrust it through a pane. A musical tinkle of glass. Then she pulled back the catch inside and forced up the sash.

With shaking legs she clambered over the sill, dragged the bundle away from the stove and over to the window — without daring to look at it — and turned off the gas. Then she unlocked the door, hurried downstairs to the telephone, and dialled feverishly for the doctor.

She would say nothing on the 'phone, but urged him to come at once. Dr. Paget, when he arrived, commended her warmly for her presence of mind and discretion. Between them they carried the fragile little wisp into a room that chanced conveniently to be vacant just then.

Dr. Paget waited at her bedside till Florence came round.

'Now, whatever made you do a thing like that?' he said gently.

She burst into tears and shook her head.

'Come now, why?' he urged. 'What is it?'

She conveyed, between sobs, that it was the utter hopelessness of everything.

'Not at all,' said Dr. Paget firmly. 'You're getting along very nicely. Nothing to be depressed about. I've had a very satisfactory report from the specialist,' he invented, 'very satisfactory . . . What did he say to you?' he added cautiously.

'Oh, I don't know. That I must get away.'

'Quite right — quite right. Wish I could go away for a bit. Where are you going?'

That was exactly what all the trouble was about! And then it all tumbled out: how beastly Phoebe had been, how unfair it all was, how she couldn't possibly go away alone to some strange place, and so on and so on.

'What a fuss about nothing.' Dr. Paget patted her hand to show that, though he was being stern, he was not really cross. 'Now, you're not to bother about it anymore. I shall fix up everything for you myself. I know the very place for you — with some good friends of mine who'll see that you're properly looked after.'

'Oh! I couldn't stay with strangers,' she cried in horror.

'Of course you can. And they're used to looking after people. You needn't meet the other guests unless you feel like it.'

'What is it?' she asked suspiciously. 'A nursing-home? I won't go to a nursing-home.'

'A sort of nursing-home — more of a rest home, really — for people who want a quiet holiday and don't want to be bothered with hotel life. The people who run it are very nice and the food is good. Now, I'll fix it up for you, and all you'll have to do is to pack up a few things. You needn't bother about the journey, I'll run you down by car.'

'Oh, I can't, I can't! Don't make me. Let me be.'

'You know, you can be imprisoned for what you've done,' he said sternly.

She crumpled up at once. 'All right. I'll go. Where is it?' she said weakly.

'Brighton. Now, there are to be no more naughty tricks! Promise . . . ? Good girl!'

Mrs. Bowles did the packing for her next day and, though Florence protested that she felt too ill to travel, helped her dress, for Mrs. Bowles had her instructions. Florence said nothing when Mrs. Bowles told her that Phoebe had rung up the evening before.

'She asked you to give her a call,' she reported.

Florence snorted and tightened her mouth relentlessly.

The day was crisp and bright with sunshine, and there was little traffic on the roads. They bowled along briskly, Florence staring morosely out of the window at her own wretched thoughts, anxiety shadowing her narrow face and chilling her hands.

The doctor drew up his car at the beginning of Hove, before a secluded residence in a quiet road ten minutes' walk from the sea.

'Here we are,' he said cheerily, and helped her out.

Florence's heart misgave her as she looked at it, but she followed the doctor up the path.

3

The Kind Lady

A 'sort of' nursing-home, he had said, and she had thought — she wasn't sure now quite what she had thought or expected, but certainly not nurses; there seemed to be nurses everywhere. They welcomed her too brightly, for one thing; and for another, she disliked the quiet ominous rustling of their clothes.

Dr. Paget patted her on the back and disappeared with a wave of his hand into the Matron's sanctum. She called good-bye to him yearningly, and turned obediently to follow a nurse up, up, up, to the very top of the narrow house, into a small room very barely and hideously furnished. Eighty years ago, when the house was first built, this room had been used as the night-nursery of some Victorian family, and there were still the bars over the windows.

'I expect you'd like to go straight to bed, wouldn't you?' said the nurse, with a cast-iron smile of sympathy. 'You must be tired after your journey. I'll just get you a hot-bottle, and then I'll come and unpack for you.' She slid out of the door.

Florence, dumb with dread, stared at the bars. She knew what *they* meant all right. She'd been trapped! She felt dizzy and sick with panic. The walls crowded in on her . . . there was no air . . . she struggled with a desire to scream, but she mustn't let them know she was afraid, or she would never get away. Suddenly she wondered if the nurse had locked the door after her and she darted across the room, wrenching numbly at the stiff handle. It opened. Thank God!

'Not undressed yet?' said the nurse gaily. 'There's a slowcoach! I'd better help you.'

As she advanced, Florence shrank back quivering, speechless, her eyes wild. She hated to be touched by anyone, but her dread of a scene, some horrid vision of herself cowering in some dark corner in a strait-waistcoat if she should not behave 'properly', made her suffer the nurse's clean, chilly fingers against her skin meekly. The nurse chattered briskly, inquisitive as a bird. But answer came there none. She was too canny to let what she said be used in evidence against her: and there might be Dictaphones in those walls. She remained stonily silent.

Finally, the nurse bustled away and left her lying stiff and flat in the narrow bed; unrelaxed, staring up at the ceiling, and plotting, plotting, plotting . . .

Every hour or so, they peeped in on her archly to inquire if there was anything she wanted. They brought her Bovril and Horlicks, and watery little messes of steamed fish and rice pudding. She slept, and woke when it was dark, to see strange shapes about her that made her heart throb till she remembered, and saw narrow beams of light squinting around the room as people passed softly along the corridor. She lay awake a long time revolving her anxious thoughts and listening in dread for maniacal screams from the other inmates . . . and, in her contrariness, finding the utter silence even more ominous. Presently she slept again and woke to the raw misery of dawn and all the screeching birds, who seemed to be inside her head pecking her poor nerves to bits. Tears ran down her cheeks. That relieved her inner tension somewhat, and a little later a wickedly strong cup of early-morning tea helped to revive her spirits.

She felt wretched, but all the same she forced herself to get up, for the sooner she knew the lie of the land the better, as also the system on which the place was run.

Just as she was combing her hair into some kind of order, she heard a shriek — or, rather, a cadenza of shrieks — which conveyed such anguish and terror that she stopped breathing altogether while she listened. *What could it mean?* Her heart sank. And then that alarming silence again. Were they torturing someone? Could such things occur in the present day?

She must find out what it was. Yet when the nurse brought in her lunch, she could not bring herself to mention it — for fear of what she would hear if they told her the truth; for fear that they might lie to her, leaving her free to imagine some nameless horror; for fear also of giving herself away, and letting them know that she knew what sort of a place she had come to.

So she sat quiet and sullen as usual. But the food stuck in her throat, and when she came to fetch the tray away, the nurse commented brightly: 'Didn't fancy your dinner today? Now why was that, I wonder? Don't you like sweetbreads . . . ? Mmm! You must do better than that . . . '

The next day, she asked if she was allowed out of her room, and when they told her she was she wandered gingerly about the house, wondering fearfully, like Bluebeard's wife, what horrors lay behind all those closed and silent doors.

She saw, from a ground floor window, one old lady, wrapped up like a winter caterpillar, sitting in a corner of the green fence-bordered strip they called a garden, knitting and mumbling to herself; and later she saw a very thin young man with a crumpled face leaning on a small stout nurse and talking vivaciously. Those were the only patients she ever saw.

In a few days she had observed the main points in their simple routine, and it was quite easy, one morning after they had brought round the mid-morning drinks, for her to stuff her purse into the leg of her bloomers and hatless and coatless — going so obviously nowhere in particular — stroll quietly down the long staircase and out of the house.

Once beyond the gate, she turned to the right and ran towards the main road as fast as she could force her legs to carry her. It was dangerous to run, it looked suspicious and attracted notice, she knew; but she dared not linger in those parts too long lest she should meet a nurse on her way to the post-box or some such thing. She glanced over her shoulder anxiously.

An orange cab advanced slowly down the road, holding such promise of freedom and security and privacy in its clumsy lines that, without hesitation, she sprang into the roadway, wrenched open its door before it had even come to a standstill, and jumped in, crying: 'To the station.' She shrank back against the slippery upholstery, trembling with excitement.

The fare was only a few shillings, and she paid and hurried into Brighton station. She rapped on the ticket-seller's window.

'A single to London,' she said. And saw with dismay that she had only a few coins left after paying the taxi, and there was no note in her purse. There lay the green slip of pasteboard. And here lay a two-shilling piece, a sixpence, a few pennies, and a brass threepenny bit. It was not enough, she forced her startled mind to acknowledge, and with trembling fingers she picked them up and shut them in her purse, not even hearing the clerk's rude words . . . The station was dark and wavy, with people suddenly shouting behind her, and noisy wheels . . . She had to be quiet, she had to think, and she descended into the murky cloakroom that smelt damp and stuffy at the same time.

She stood there for goodness knew how long, hearing and not hearing the sharply banging doors, seeing and not seeing the women passing to and fro and prinking before the shadowy mirrors, so hard was she trying to imagine what her next move could be, how she was possibly to extricate herself from this dilemma of pennilessness and estrangement. There was nowhere she could go — except back to 'that place', and to that she cried, 'No, never!' inwardly — and nothing she could sell.

A voice said gently: 'You're in trouble, aren't you? Can I help?'

Kind blue eyes looked into hers. Beneath the comfortable brown felt hat, the ruddy weather-beaten face was framed in soft white hair. A small Cairn snuggled under her arm. The woman had a friendly smile. Florence stared at her, weighing her up suspiciously; it might be another trick — but the dog gave her confidence: people who loved animals . . .

'You poor dear!' exclaimed the woman, with a wealth of sympathy in her tone.

Florence now disgraced herself by bursting into tears. Never had she been more in need of a bosom to weep on, and here was one to hand; she could not resist taking advantage of it. The woman tut-tutted soothingly, and muttered that she looked absolutely done in and must have something to eat, and carried her off to the buffet.

Mrs. Jolly she said her name was, as Florence mopped up her tears and sipped her tea; and Belinda was the name of the pretty little dog she fondled on her lap. She had been watching Florence in the mirror, and never, she said, had she seen anyone in such obvious distress. She was not the sort of person to interfere with other people as a rule, but she felt she simply couldn't let her go.

'I — I haven't any money,' said Florence. 'I don't mean that exactly, I have got plenty at home, but not here, and I want to get to London — at once.'

But it wasn't as easy as that. The lady asked questions — oh, very kindly, not at all suspiciously; but still, Florence had to think up suitable answers, for it would never do just to blurt out the ugly truth. And yet her story could not have been very convincing, for suddenly Mrs. Jolly laughed cheerily and said: 'Suppose you tell me the truth. Even if you *were* called to London suddenly from your holiday, you know, there's no reason not to have on a hat and coat. The weather is not as clement as that. Come, what are you afraid of? I can't believe you've done anything so very dreadful. Is it the police — ? No? I'm glad of that. But you *are* running away from someone — or something — aren't you? Why not tell me about it?'

'They're trying to shut me up,' Florence whispered. And when Mrs. Jolly did not seem to understand, she added: 'They're trying to put me away. They say they say I'm mad.'

'Good gracious! I've never heard of such a thing!' Mrs. Jolly looked shocked.

'You don't think I'm mad, do you?' said Florence anxiously.

Mrs. Jolly reassured her vehemently.

'But what are your relatives about, allowing such a thing?'

'I'm an orphan,' Florence explained, with a three-cornered smile.

'But haven't you anyone who could be responsible for you, a guardian or anyone?' persisted Mrs. Jolly.

'No, no one at all. I'm alone in the world. So it's easy, isn't it?'

'Yes, I suppose so. How dreadful! But what I don't understand is why anyone should want to get you out of the way. What good can it do them?'

Florence looked at her helplessly. 'I don't know.'

'Is it money, do you think? Have you any money?'

'A little,' said Florence cautiously. She was always prudish about money, as though the word was obscene in some way.

'Well, I don't know, I'm sure,' remarked Mrs. Jolly. 'But it seems a very terrible thing to me. And I think you were a very plucky girl to run away like that.'

'If only I'd had enough money to get right away, I'd be safe by now. I'm so afraid they'll get hold of me again.'

'They shan't do that; don't worry,' said Mrs. Jolly, with a firmness that sounded delightful to Florence. She warmed immediately to her.

The very first thing to do, Mrs. Jolly

declared, was to get her belongings away, then there would be time enough to make further plans. No, of course she did not expect Florence to go and get them. All she wanted of her was the address. And when Florence wrote it down for her, she frowned and asked Florence if she was sure that it was a mental home, because she had always understood it to be a home for old ladies or something of that sort.

'Absolutely positive,' said Florence emphatically, for she was by now completely convinced of the truth of her story, which ran now on the vaguely familiar lines of the missing heiress being kidnapped for some nefarious purpose by her enemies.

Mrs. Jolly's thoughts were running on quite different lines . . . Florence would have a cheque book, she supposed, among her belongings; and once she had that she would be all right.

Florence blushed. 'I don't bank my money, as a matter of fact . . . It's a long story, and I won't go into it now, but I receive my money weekly. I budget pretty carefully, and what I don't spend gets put on one side. I have a Savings Account.'

'Well, it doesn't signify either way. I expect you have your account book with you, then. You don't think I'm being impertinent, do you? I'm only trying to help.'

Again Florence shook her head.

'Oh, don't let's bother about it now,' said Mrs. Jolly. 'The first thing to do is to make you feel safe, you poor little soul. Now, I'm going to take you to a nice comfortable hotel — '

'Not too fashionable,' flashed the other, meaning *not too expensive.*

' — Of course not! — while I collect your luggage for you. Then we shall see.'

'It *is* good of you to take all this trouble,' murmured Florence, comparing this kindly stranger bitterly in her heart with Phoebe.

'Think no more about it. No — no, I shall pay for this,' insisted Mrs. Jolly munificently, counting out coppers on the marble table.

Mrs. Jolly found her a mean little

boarding-house near Kemp Town, whis-pering that it was good enough for a day or two, dear. It was called the Belleview Hotel, and the name adequately indicated its tawdriness. But then, as Mrs. Jolly pointed out, how many places were there that would take in a half-dressed stranger without any luggage? She went away then, promising to return soon, and telling her to be sure not to worry.

Florence was shown upstairs into a slit of a room that held a bed, a chair, a wash-stand, and space to slip between them sideways. The walls were papered alarmingly with scarlet and magenta parakeets and yellow roses.

As soon as Florence was alone once more, she felt frightened. She sat on the edge of the creaking bed and counted twenty-three red parakeets, twenty-four purple ones, and nine yellow roses. Then she closed her eyes. Suppose this was yet another delusion? Mrs. Jolly was probably going to steal her luggage. No, that she could never believe. Finally, she ventured into the dingy corridor outside, peering through the dimness at each passing face and trying to pluck up the courage to ask if there was a writing-room she could use; for it might not be a bad idea to write to Mrs. Bowles and ask her to send on her Savings Book, which she would find in the top left-hand drawer of her chest. She did not at all care for the idea of Mrs. Bowles seeing exactly what her savings were, but that could not be helped.

There were only two sheets of paper and three envelopes in the varnished holder, and she timidly took one of each and sat down. The letterhead came nearly halfway down the page, bristling with the information that it was a first-class establishment, that afternoon tea was served in the palm lounge, that all the rooms boasted electricity, and that it was near the sea. *All lies*, thought Florence acidly, and took up the scratchy pen.

★ ★ ★

Mrs. Jolly walked briskly along the promenade in the sharp spring sunshine. Her tweeds, though rather worn and tasteless in cut, were plainly of good quality. She looked what she was — a lady. And this was as well, because she was going into the Hotel Metropole, and she did not want people to come rushing up as soon as she appeared to inquire what she wanted. She walked assuredly and unobtrusively into the large and sunlit writing-room and, seating herself at one of the desks, began to write.

The letter was to the Matron of the nursing-home and written in a rather florid hand, purporting to be from a Miss Emma Brown, who was staying at the above address and had that very morning met her niece, Miss Florence Brown, in the town. While praising highly the Matron's reputable establishment, she yet preferred to have her niece under her own eye, and to this end she had made arrangements for her to stay at the Hotel Metropole, and she — Miss Emma Brown — would be greatly obliged if her niece's things could be packed up and given to the bearer: together, of course, with her account. She remained theirs very truly.

Having stuck down the envelope and

addressed it, she left the ornate building for a dull grey box of a house a few streets away. This was the office of the District Messengers. A lout was dispatched with instructions, and Mrs. Jolly sat down to await results. He was not gone so very long, and when he returned he carried with him two shoddy fibre suitcases and a cardboard box.

Mrs. Jolly did not go straight back to the Belleview Hotel. She rang Florence up and told her the good news.

'I won't bring them round just yet, in case I'm being followed, you see. I don't think I am, for one minute; I'm sure they don't suspect anything, but it is as well to be on the safe side, don't you think?'

Florence was relieved and wanted to know when and where she could come to collect them.

'Oh, you mustn't come and fetch them,' Mrs. Jolly protested. 'You must lie low for a few days at least, till your money comes and you can get away. I think it would be most unwise for you to be seen outside the hotel till then . . . Do you think I'm a bit of a scaremonger? Perhaps

I am . . . But you needn't worry about your things — you shall have them in a little while; I only want time to throw any possible followers off the track a little. What is the number of your room? I'll bring them straight up when I come. You stay there and wait for me.' And she cut short Florence's complaints by repeating that it was only for a little while.

It was fortunate that Mrs. Jolly had inquired about the number of her room, for there was no one in the office, no staff anywhere to be seen, when she arrived with the suitcases. That was a frequent state of affairs at the Belleview Hotel: perhaps they considered thieves as unlikely on the whole as potential visitors.

Mrs. Jolly was forced to admit that it was hardly ideal. And yet, she reminded Florence, she might complain as she pleased that all those gaudy parrots gave her claustrophobia — there were no bars over the windows. That surely was something to be grateful for.

Florence tried to be grateful. It wasn't easy, when all the colours were clashing in your brain so that you couldn't breathe.

'I have a plan,' said Mrs. Jolly shyly. 'I don't know whether it will appeal to you,' she added with a blush. 'The fact is — I haven't told you anything about myself, have I? My husband — dear soul! — he's dead now — was a doctor. I was a nurse before I married and we worked in the same hospital, and that was how we met. So you see I know quite a bit about looking after people. And sometimes I do take an invalid, or an old lady who needs attention, as a P.G. in my little house. I'm quite glad to, for now that I'm alone I am often lonely. And I thought . . . it occurred to me . . . '

'That I might, you mean,' said Florence, with a look that was almost eager.

'I don't see why not, if you like the idea. It wouldn't cost you any more than you are paying here, and less than you paid at 'that place', and you would be getting proper attention and good, well-cooked food, and rest without loneliness — which I always say is very important. Mind you, I don't want you to feel that you've got to accept, but if you really have nowhere else to go and no one to stay with . . . '

'I think it would be lovely,' said Florence, 'if you could bear to have someone like me around. It's most awfully good of you. I can't think why you should take all this trouble over me.'

'Believe me, it's a pleasure, dear,' Mrs. Jolly assured her, her blue eyes shining warmly. 'Now, you'll stay quietly here like a good girl for a day or two, for I have one or two things to see to, and you must wait for your money before you can leave here: and then I'll come and fetch you.'

The next few days were wretched for Florence, worse in a way than the nightmare days in the nursing-home, for her surroundings were so intolerably sordid now, and the food was uneatable and the boredom excruciating and unrelieved. Yet she stayed; even after she received the registered letter from Mrs. Bowles containing her Savings Book, she stayed, waiting to hear from Mrs. Jolly, till she feared that it was one more prank of a malign fate and that she was never to hear of her again. She was glad when, on the third day of her ordeal, she was called to the telephone to hear Mrs. Jolly's comfortable voice. She was ready, if Florence was. Florence said she could be, except for the little matter of her bill. Oh no, she had her bank book all right, it was just a question of drawing it out, and Mrs. Jolly had said it was not safe for her. Now Mrs. Jolly assured her on that point, and she agreed that it probably would be safe enough for her to run round to the nearest post office and draw out three pounds, which should be enough to pay her bill.

'Will it suit you if I call for you about ten-thirty tomorrow, then? Or would that be too early? That'll just give us nice time to get settled in before lunch, if that suits you all right.'

Florence nervously said it did suit her.

'Fine!' said Mrs. Jolly. 'Till tomorrow, then. And cheer up, you silly old thing, you're not going to be executed — yet!'

4

A Cottage in the Country

Florence had not unpacked in the first place, so she had not the nervous strain of repacking, and she was ready when Mrs. Jolly called for her. A small boy of uncertain age and occupation, and a face as red and shiny as a rosehip in October, lugged her belongings downstairs.

She paid the bill, and the sour woman at the desk with a voice like a steel file receipted it grimly. Now, where was Mrs. Jolly? Outside, waiting in such a nice little dark-green car; she had not even known that her friend had a car; that was a jolly surprise! And that was a pun that she must remember to tell her friend. For her spirits had risen considerably in the pleasant sunlight with the wide blue horizons all round her, after being cooped up in that dreadful room for days and days.

She watched Jim, the red-faced boy, stow the luggage in the shoe at the back, and handed him sixpence for his pains, which he tossed up in the air derisively, while she climbed in beside Mrs. Jolly and — rather nervously, for she wasn't good with animals — took Belinda on her lap.

It was a lovely day. Beyond the downs that curved an incredible pink against the blue-streaked sky, lay a dark blur of trees and roofs in the midst of a broad, flat expanse of faded green, quilted here and there with silver and blue ribbons of water and rough woolly hedges.

'That,' said Mrs. Jolly, 'is Patchet.'

Patchet was the name of her village: one of those typically English villages which appear to have been nipped in the bud of time somewhere about the age of Queen Elizabeth and remained in that period ever since. It was quaint. At the end of the settlement, Mrs. Jolly turned down a narrow lane, and on between dark hedges just bursting into bud. A few minutes more and she drew up before a quaint, tumbledown cottage.

Mrs. Jolly led her up the little crooked path through the wild profusion of the small golden flowers of spring that spangled the waving grass.

'Isn't it sweet?' she demanded, and Florence agreed that it was. But it was somehow not at all the kind of setting she had pictured for her friend. She had imagined a rather solid modern villa, with everything very neat and good-style. Surely this was not where she had lived with her husband. This was nothing like a doctor's house. And inside it was even more surprising. It didn't even have electric light, though there was a telephone, she noticed — of course a doctor would have to be on the telephone.

Downstairs there was the kitchen and the parlour and a little 'den', used for God knew what. Upstairs were the two bedrooms, a murky bathroom and a capacious linen cupboard. The garden was pretty, but untended, even Florence's untutored eye could see.

'I've let it get terribly out of hand,' sighed Mrs. Jolly. 'I shall really have to pull my socks up now you're here.

Gardening is my hobby, though you mightn't think it to look out there.'

Although they were so far from other people, although Florence was so unused to the quiet of country life, although there seemed nothing whatever to do, she was not dull. For one thing, it did Florence a power of good to have someone actually noticing her, taking an interest in her, considering her. And then Mrs. Jolly positively would not allow her to keep talking about her symptoms and how ill she felt; she would shut her up firmly and change the subject: and Mrs. Jolly could be quite an entertaining companion when she chose. She was a good plain cook, too, who enjoyed cooking because she relished her food — which was more than poor dyspeptic Florence did, by the way. And really, when the lamps were lit and the curtains drawn, it was as snug as any place you could wish to see, and Florence felt quite 'real' and grown-up sitting by the fireside and having an interesting conversation with her friend — just like other people did.

When Mrs. Jolly had temporarily used

up her store of anecdotes, Florence began questioning her avidly about the very many photographs hanging about the room, for she was passionately eager now to know every detail of her friend's life, wanting to identify herself utterly with her if that were possible.

It was a fascinating inquiry. There was Alice, Mrs. Jolly's favourite sister, with her hair pulled low over her forehead and a bandeau round her head, looking archly over the top of a tennis racquet.

'But she doesn't look a bit like you,' protested Florence.

'There's no law that sisters have to look alike,' laughed Mrs. Jolly.

'Well, no, that's true. Phoebe and I — ' She stopped abruptly.

'Phoebe?' said Mrs. Jolly wonderingly. 'I haven't heard you mention that name before, have I? Who's that?'

'Phoebe was my sister,' Florence growled reluctantly.

'Was? Is she dead?'

'She's dead to me,' said Florence sternly.

'I didn't even know you had a sister

— ' Mrs. Jolly sounded the least bit hurt.

'We quarrelled.' That was enough of that. Drop the subject quickly. 'Tell me more about Alice,' she begged.

'Alice was the family beauty,' said Mrs. Jolly.

'Oh no!' cried Florence.

'Yes, I was the ugly duckling. And I remember one time . . . ' The story trickled out its length, with Florence hanging on every golden word of it.

'And this?' asked Florence, pointing to a handsome laughing man standing on the overmantel with folded arms.

'My husband,' said Mrs. Jolly, and blew him a little kiss.

Florence could not restrain a tiny pang of jealousy at that sign of an affection that endured beyond the grave, and said sharply: 'I thought you said his name was John?'

'Well?'

'This says, 'Your loving Bobby'.'

'He *was* my loving Bobby. That was *my* name for him, I always called him that because I thought the name suited him far better than John. Besides . . . John

Jolly! 'Dr. John Jolly' sounds perfectly ridiculous. Don't you think he looks a Bobby?'

Florence agreed that perhaps he did. Then there was her Aunt Dorothy rising wistfully out of a nest of chiffon. She was to have been a singer; a lovely girl, they said, only she died of galloping consumption quite unexpectedly. A terrible tragedy.

The photograph game went on.

And when that was ended there was supper by the fire. By the time that was eaten and cleared away, Florence was quite tired. It had been a big day for her. And Mrs. Jolly packed her off to bed while she did the washing-up.

The next day was heavy with potential rain, which showered down intermittently without lightening the atmosphere. So Florence was confined to the house; it was not to be expected that she should go for a country walk in that sort of weather. Belinda had to have her paws wiped every time she came in from the garden.

While Mrs. Jolly ran the car down to the village to get some stores she needed,

Florence languidly dusted the parlour, pausing a long time before each portrait and reliving what her friend had told her about them the night before. Lovely Alice, tragic Dorothy, redoubtable Edith, brainy Cyril, Harold the scamp, and so on. What a fascinating family! She wanted to know more and more, the better to understand her friend . . . Her husband, now. He was awfully good-looking, and Florence had taken a most unreasonable dislike to him. She picked up the frame and slid the photo out. What large, bold writing, not a bit like a doctor's. 'Your loving Bobby'. Oh, and here, hidden by the edge of the frame before, was the date . . . but — but — that was only last year! That was absurd! That could not be. Why, Dr. Jolly had died years ago. Mrs. Jolly had not said exactly when, but she had made it clear enough that it was a long time ago. There must be some mistake.

All the same, Florence put it hastily back in its place with an unaccountable feeling of guilt. A little sensation of fear, which she did not analyse, worried the top of her head: a vague feeling of discomfort, of something wrong some-where, a sudden loosening of the stays of security that persisted as she moved from room to room with her duster . . .

The rest of the day was fairly uneventful. But they were neither of them bored, for they still had plenty to discover about one another. It was Florence's turn to be questioned; and she was often hard put to it to answer Mrs. Jolly's pointed queries without telling the truth. There were some things she was determined Mrs. Jolly should not know, from vanity rather than because she had anything that needed to be concealed. Hoggers, she had to confess, the inglorious optical lens and artificial eye manufacturers, but she improved her own position there, as she did so, from secretary to Chief Executive of the Export Department. It sounded grand and she guessed that however little she knew about the un-genteel occupa-tion of making glass eyes (and in twenty years her work had been all on the clerical side) she would still have the advantage over Mrs. Jolly. But about Phoebe she remained a clam.

'She was an actress,' she said. As if that explained everything. And, 'I'd rather not talk about her,' when Mrs. Jolly persisted.

Mrs. Jolly, who had planned to garden all the afternoon, was prevented by a heavy downpour which lasted till nightfall. Mrs. Jolly was rather more disappointed than the occasion warranted. Still, her habitual good-humour was not marred for long. It was a good opportunity to get some of her neglected business affairs tidied up. She was a terribly lazy person, she told Florence with a wry smile.

'I'll be as quiet as a mouse,' said Florence, watching her friend settle herself with a satchel full of papers and a fountain pen, and perch a pair of horned-rimmed spectacles on her nose.

Later on Mrs. Jolly looked up over the top of her glasses and said: 'I wonder if you'd mind witnessing my signature to various deeds — I'm selling out some stock, and one thing and another — and it would save a trip down to the lawyers and eight and sixpence, or whatever it is now.'

Florence naturally was only too glad to

oblige. Nothing very arduous about that. Of course, she knew one should never sign anything without reading it first (she had not worked in an office for twenty years for nothing), but you could hardly sit down and read a friend's private business papers, all those details to do with her income and such; it would be cheek, wouldn't it? Besides being excessively tedious to wade through some two dozen papers. Mrs. Jolly did not offer to let her read them, for one thing; she held the papers and indicated where Florence should sign, and she signed. She was not to suppose her death warrant was among them.

5

Suspicion

The following day was fine and clear and as soon as the house was cleaned, Mrs. Jolly hurried into the garden, working assiduously till lunch time, clearing the tangled mass of weeds, scrutinizing every plant personally, as it were, and generally tidying up.

Florence suggested going for a walk; the village was a little too far there and back, she thought, but a little ramble round-about would be pleasant. However, being physically lazy from anaemia and her city life, she did not need much encouragement from Mrs. Jolly to stay with her in the garden. She would not allow Florence to tire herself by helping her, but said it was nice to have her to talk to. Although she seemed to have worked wonders in her little patch of ground, even to Florence's ignorant eyes,

Mrs. Jolly did not appear satisfied with her day's work. She sat with her catalogues surrounding her that evening, making out her seed lists and looking things up in gardening books. And Florence noticed that the lists were not definitive and either grew too long or did not grow at all; while more than anything else Mrs. Jolly studied an old tattered book that smelt positively mouldy, a frown making a straight line of her thick white eyebrows.

The next day Florence did not feel so well; her nerves were on edge. It was the kind of day that did not agree with her, that was too crude for her worn physique. Ragged clouds blown across a harsh blue sky that seemed limitlessly high; sunlight as sharp as knives, the cardboard landscape standing out stiffly with a firm blue outline; and a boisterous wind shouting in the trees and kicking up the dust in the roadway, which was in itself enough to give anyone a headache.

'Depression over Iceland,' remarked Mrs. Jolly, to her surly companion at the breakfast table. 'Probably rain tonight, then you'll feel better. It's the falling barometer, you see, that makes you feel like that.'

'How do you know?' said Florence, not because she disbelieved her but because she wished to be disagreeable.

'A doctor's wife picks up these little hints, you know. Besides, I've been a nurse, I told you. I can see when people feel rotten.'

Florence shut up then, a little ashamed of her evident irritability.

It was later that morning that Florence flew to the foot of the stairs to call in an urgent whisper to Mrs. Jolly that there was a lady coming up the path.

'A lady?' Mrs. Jolly glanced quickly out of the bedroom window, shielding herself from view with the curtain. Little enough she could see — a mushroom felt, a dark tweed overcoat, the edge of a shopping basket. And the bell rang. Useless to pretend they were out when the car was right under her nose; moreover, she would be certain to call again another time and then she might have the misfortune to find only Florence in the house, and that would never do. The bell rang again.

'Shall I open?' floated up to her in an anxious whisper.

'No, no, I'm coming. It's all right,' she called back softly, smoothing her hands over her short white hair as she hurried downstairs. She seized Florence by the shoulders and said, with her agreeable firmness: 'Look here, if you're not feeling up to the mark you won't want to be bothered with strangers — and this woman's a fearful bore. Why don't you bunk upstairs and take a couple of aspirin and lie down for a bit.' She pushed her gently but firmly towards the stairs as she spoke, and Florence was halfway up the stairs before Mrs. Jolly turned to open the door in answer to the third peal of the bell.

'I'm so sorry,' said Mrs. Jolly prettily, as she opened the door.

And, 'I'm afraid I've come at a rather inconvenient hour,' the stranger answered.

And that was all that Florence heard just then. Quietly she closed her bedroom door.

It was nice of Mrs. Jolly to be so thoughtful for her, she really did not feel like talking to strangers — not that she ever did. It was different with Mrs. Jolly; Mrs. Jolly was her friend. And so kind . . . Or had she merely wanted her out of the way and used tact to get rid of her without hurting her feelings? Perhaps she wanted to talk to the woman privately. Perhaps the woman was a great friend of hers. Perhaps Mrs. Jolly was ashamed of her new friend, who certainly wasn't anything to boast of in the way of looks or brains or position.

'And who is Miss Brown?' Florence imagined the stranger asking. 'Oh, just a miserable little creature I picked up on Brighton station. She was destitute and half-dotty; I think she was going to throw herself on the rails,' Mrs. Jolly would say. And they would laugh.

Florence flushed heavily and clenched her fists. If they were talking about her! And with beating heart crept downstairs to listen.

'Oh, not for long — I hope,' she heard Mrs. Jolly say. 'Though it really is not so bad here considering how primitive it is. You see, I hope to settle in the district, and I'm driving round the countryside looking for a house to buy, and this makes quite a serviceable base for operations. Yes, I particularly want to buy, I'm sick of renting houses — so unsatisfactory — and I want to own my own property. I suppose you don't know of anywhere suitable?'

'What type of place?' asked the visitor.

'Smallish, a villa . . . say, three bedrooms . . . for me and my son. No, he's not here. I'm alone at present. Oh, I'm never lonely — there's doggy for company.'

Then something Florence could not catch. Then:

'But you must . . . Not at all, I always do at this time in the morning.' And the door opened suddenly, right in her face.

At sight of Florence crouching there, Mrs. Jolly drew in her breath sharply and closed the door quickly behind her. Her face was very red and her blue eyes were bright with anger. 'What are you doing here?' she said roughly, through her teeth, speaking as though Florence were a disobedient child. Florence shrank back and stared at her, too astonished for words. But perhaps it was only a trick of the light, for the next instant Mrs. Jolly was her customary bland and smiling self.

'I — I came down to get — to get a glass of water for my aspirin,' Florence improvised.

'You made me jump out of my skin,' declared Mrs. Jolly. 'Don't let her catch you here. I'm just going to make her a cup of tea and then I'll get rid of her afterwards. Run along and have a nice rest, dear.'

And Florence ran along.

A thoroughly sound woman, was the verdict of the vicar's wife as, her duty-call ended, she walked away. And yet, niggled her mind, I swear I heard voices when she went to make the tea, and she distinctly told me she was alone. I daresay she has a char for a couple of hours a week. And, satisfied with that solution, she dismissed the matter from her thoughts.

As for Florence, she thought what she thought. She could be as mum as a cat when she chose, and not even Mrs. Jolly could decipher what lay behind that peaky face. She wasn't such a fool as to ask for an explanation of what she had heard, and Mrs. Jolly was far too clever to embark on one unsolicited.

'Do you know,' said Florence over dinner, with a little laugh, 'I dreamt of Ethel last night and how she put the mouse in the governess's bed, and all that, like you told me the other day.' And she held up the photograph of 'Edith'. 'Was she good-looking? She doesn't look as attractive as Alice,' she pattered on.

'Ethel?' said Mrs. Jolly rather absently. 'She was not exactly pretty, but she was a great success with everyone because she was so gay.'

'Sad that she died.'

'Yes. She could have married anybody.'

'I thought you said she did marry and went to live in Borneo,' snapped down Florence accusingly.

'So she did. She married a missionary. A rotten life. She could have had anyone. Though she always said she was happy enough with Herbert in Borneo.'

'Was that before or after she died?' said Florence astutely. Mrs. Jolly looked bewildered for a moment, and then burst into a Homeric roar of laughter. Florence flushed, aware that she had made a complete ass of herself. 'Did she go to Borneo before or after she died . . . ? Oh, that's rich that is!' gasped Mrs. Jolly, wiping her eyes.

'I didn't mean that,' growled Florence sulkily, hating to be laughed at, never able to see a joke against herself and, on this occasion, oversensitive to the importance of her slip, brought about through trying to be too clever.

As usual after a moral mishap of this sort, she experienced a complete *volte face*. Now she was ashamed of herself for her beastly neurotic suspicions. It just showed she wasn't normal and couldn't be trusted to behave decently. Eavesdropping, which was a disgusting thing to do in itself, and then trying to make out people were liars just because you didn't quite understand what was said. And suppose Mrs. Jolly had let her call Edith Ethel and hadn't corrected her, that probably only meant that she was too well-mannered to keep interrupting and putting her right. She wanted to fling herself on Mrs. Jolly in maudlin self-reproach and confess the beastly thoughts she had been harbouring against her. Only, of course, it wouldn't do. Mrs. Jolly might not understand, she might be offended, and that would be terrible. The rest of the meal was eaten mostly in silence, each so busy with her own thoughts.

At one point Mrs. Jolly broke the silence to say that she had to go out for a little while that afternoon, if Florence did not object to being left alone. That was quite all right, Florence said absently. Florence was saying something over and over again in her head, unable to make up her mind whether to voice it or not. At last she said timidly, in a voice that sounded very loud and false in her own ears:

'Have you been a widow long, Mrs. Jolly?'

'Six years in September,' sighed Mrs. Jolly promptly.

Then why, Florence wanted to ask — but was very careful not to — why is the photo of your husband signed with last year's date? Answer me that, Mrs. Jolly, if you can, she addressed her silently, with a mixture of gloom and triumph . . . for if it was nice to be right, it was not nice to be right about nasty things. And all this thinking made her headache much worse.

So Florence was quite glad to see Mrs. Jolly pulling on her old felt hat before the mirror. She needed to be alone to reach some definite conclusion about this strange matter. The Cairn rushed round in excited circles, barking hysterically.

'Does oo want to come wiz muzzer, zen?' said Mrs. Jolly in her special Belinda voice, picking her up and kissing her black nose. Belinda peeked up cutely through her fringe and licked her mistress's cheek. 'Oh, I could eat you to bits, you precious thing,' she remarked, squeezing her violently.

Florence looked on with distaste and a feeling of inferiority. One ought to love animals, of course; all English people always did, it was a sign of character; and yet to see people slopping over dogs did somehow repel her. She could not but think she was more lovable, more worthy of kisses than that little creature hardly more animate than a toy. She supposed vaguely that she would feel differently in the matter if she owned a pet herself. She could not acknowledge the resentment she felt as jealousy, because she did not recognize it as such; she was unaware of her subconscious thought processes.

It was all very well, she said to herself, after they had gone, it was all very well to scold herself one minute for her stupid notions and then to switch round and be all wary and suspicious the next. One had to be sensible and look for — look for . . . now what was it one had to look for? A motive, of course.

She was naturally over-suspicious, she knew; that was part of her sick condition. But she remembered as clearly as anything that man saying: 'If only people with suspicions would act on them, ninety per cent of crimes could be prevented' — or something to that effect. He may have said fifty per cent. She had been a witness in some case to do with a stolen car. Fancy, all those years ago! She had been terribly nervous. But she could still see the magistrate's wise old face leaning down to make that observation.

What had she been saying? Suspicions . . . one should act on one's suspicions. No, before that. Ah yes, motives! What motive could Mrs. Jolly possibly have? That was the line of argument. But her mind shied away from the concentrated effort required to reason it out. Concentration made her skull threaten to split apart, letting the inflamed cells burst out, quivering. Ugh! That was what it felt like, anyway.

Why should Mrs. Jolly lie to her? Come on, now. She couldn't think. Her brain refused to function. Very well, reverse the situation. What made *her* lie, for instance? If she was afraid, if there was something she particularly wished to conceal, then she lied. But Mrs. Jolly couldn't be afraid of her.

And what was there she could possibly wish to conceal?

There was probably some perfectly

reasonable explanation, Florence reassured herself for the hundredth time. But still the vague uneasiness persisted, the suggestion of innumerable hidden possibilities haunted the fringes of her consciousness. If only there was someone she could turn to, someone whose advice she could ask . . . Phoebe?

There was always Phoebe, after all. She was angry with her, but she was still her sister. She would tell her . . . yes, she would write to her. She would be perfectly fair about it, she would tell her what had happened (It would mean writing about the nursing-home, she thought doubtfully. Oh, never mind that now!) and how kind Mrs. Jolly had been. She would write it at once, while she was out of the house. With unwonted decision, she seized the pot of ink off the mantelpiece, behind Alice's photo, where Mrs. Jolly had left it yesterday, and ran up to her bedroom.

There was a pad! Here a pen! She sat down excitedly and jerked her chair up to the table. The fragile table jumped at the impact, the ink-bottle tottered, tipped over, fell and rolled, sending a broad and terrifying stream of night-blue liquid across the table. Instinctively, Florence grabbed the nearest thing to her hand to arrest its flow before it reached the edge and dripped on to the carpet.

Her promptness was commendable. It soaked up at once into the towel, staining it a delightful Prussian blue. Florence stared at it, horror-struck. Whatever would Mrs. Jolly say when she saw it? She would surely be furious. To Florence in her nervous state the ruined towel assumed the proportions of a calamity. Her heart began its uncomfortably spasmodic thumping. She would hide it. She mustn't let her see it. Should she burn it? No, there might not be time. Could she bury it? No, that was idiotic, you could hardly bury a towel! Besides, Mrs. Jolly might dig it up accidentally and then the situation would be worse than ever. The thing to do was to put it somewhere where she could not get hold of it. Get it right away from the house, thought Florence, with a hunted look in her eye. But how? Why, make a parcel of it and send it somewhere. That was a brainwave, wasn't it? But where? Well, Arkwright Road would do, wouldn't it? It could await her return there quite safely. Well, hurry then, no time to lose. And there was still the letter to Phoebe, only all the ink was spilt now.

Luckily, there was no need for her to tackle the problem of posting it; with that hour's walk to the village and back that was likely to prove too much for her meagre strength; for just as she finished tying the string round the untidy parcel, the back door bell rang and she ran down to answer it.

A small boy with a large basket full of groceries stood outside. He came in and piled up a neat mound of packages on the kitchen table, and then handed her a long bill to check. It was all correct.

'That's all right,' she said.

But he did not go. What was it he wanted?

'Seven'n tuppence 'a'penny, please, 'm.'

'Doesn't it go on the book?' she frowned.

'Naow.'

'Oh well, look, Mrs. Jolly will be down tomorrow or sometime and she'll pay them. She's not in at the moment, you see.'

'Can't leave the goods wivout the cash,' said the child implacably.

'But, good heavens — it's too ridiculous! Mrs. Jolly must have dealt with you for years. You don't think she's going to run away, do you?'

'Nuffin to do wiv me, 'm. Don't blime me, blime the boss.'

'I tell you, she'll come down and pay tomorrow. Surely you can trust her for one day, can't you, you stupid boy!'

The stupid boy remarked that only established customers were allowed goods on credit; those were his orders.

'I'll 'ave to tike 'em awiy, then,' he said stolidly.

Florence, easily flustered in a crisis, was in an agony of indecision. Should she let them go back, or should she pay for them herself? What would Mrs. Jolly expect?

'Well, I'll pay,' she said grandly. 'And if I give you twopence for yourself, do you think you could take a parcel down to the post office for me? Here, lend me your pencil a moment and I'll address it.'

Nevertheless, it was queer, she thought. How was it possible for him not to know that Mrs. Jolly was an established customer? The incident set all her doubts prowling round her mind again. She remembered the morning visitor and the lies Mrs. Jolly had told her, as if she had been a stranger. Or as if Mrs. Jolly was a stranger. Yes, it did almost seem . . . Except that that was too ridiculous even to contemplate.

Yet if it was so, she realised uneasily, then Mrs. Jolly must have some strange reason for bringing her here, it must be some kind of a . . . trap. She paced up and down her room, clasping and unclasping her damp hands spasmodically, her throat constricting with her rising panic. Without understanding why, waves of terror kept riding over her.

She caught sight of her white face in the glass.

'Florence, old girl, you're in terrible danger,' she muttered aloud. The words sounded absurd. She would have laughed had it not been for the fear in her eyes and the feeling of being a prisoner caught in a box that was slowly squeezing in on her. 'Run away!' she urged herself breathlessly. 'And where will you run to, little fool?' she asked her reflection. How she hated that narrow white face, with its silly staring eyes. In a sudden fury of self-loathing she turned the mirror's face to the wall, and ran ... But a sound made her swing round and run in the other direction, to the window. Too late now to do anything. Here was the little green Austin panting at the gate.

And as soon as Mrs. Jolly came in, with her frank face and pleasant smile, she knew she'd been a fool to worry. It was her ugly warped brain that saw all sorts of nastiness where there was only sweetness and light. There could be no one kinder, more transparently open-hearted, than Mrs. Jolly. You simply couldn't imagine her doing anything rotten. She was a sweet, a darling, vowed Florence. And she seemed so pleased to be back and asked her if she had amused herself nicely, as if she was really interested. And even Belinda sprang up and down once or twice to lick her hand.

Florence had not intended to mention the little matter of the groceries — though she certainly meant to be repaid for them at some time — but Mrs. Jolly saw them lying on the kitchen table and made some comment, so Florence recounted to her what had happened.

'That's little Victor Biggs,' said Mrs. Jolly. 'The boy's a moron. I've known him since he was a kid.'

'Well, I thought it was funny. He seemed never to have heard of you. It seemed too ridiculous to me. Still, I thought I did right to pay,' she added anxiously.

'You should have rung them up and given them what for, my dear. Pack of idiots! What can you expect with a boy who can't even read and write — at his age!'

'Fancy! Still, they are backward in the country, aren't they?'

'How old do you think he is, that boy?' said Mrs. Jolly, with a strange look. 'Ten

— ? He's eighteen if he's a day.'

After that revelation Florence was prepared to believe anything.

'You surely didn't think — '

'Oh no, of course not,' said Florence uncomfortably.

'I believe you did,' said Mrs. Jolly, scrutinizing her closely but not angrily. She laughed. 'You silly girl, now whatever made you think that?'

In the end, Florence blurted out all the little oddities that had worried her, and it was surprising how readily they were explained away. The conversation she had heard between Mrs. Jolly and the vicar's wife were some rather silly lines in a part they wanted her to play in a sketch to be performed at the Women's Institute. It was a curious coincidence that should have been the bit she heard. As for the photos, they were most of them very old-fashioned, and it was surprising how unrecognizable people became; she had often not recognized herself in an old photo, and it was easy to mistake one person for another when they were not unalike. The date on her husband's photograph, she explained, was carelessly written: it was not an eight but a three, as it happened.

'Satisfied?' asked Mrs. Jolly, without malice.

'I do feel a fool.' Florence looked contrite.

Not half such a fool as you are, thought Mrs. Jolly, as she laughed and patted her head. 'Well, I'll go and get the supper now. We may as well get it over.'

We may as well get it over, she reiterated to herself in the kitchen, as she prepared the evening meal, mincing up fresh crisp leaves, scraping and grating the roots of vegetables for a salad. She kept her gloves on as she did so, perhaps in order not to spoil her hands, those nice capable hands with the closely-pared nails; sensible hands, unvarnished, unadorned except for a blood-stone signet ring on the little finger.

The supper table looked very attractive in the firelight, with the gaily checked cloth and the bright-coloured china. And on their plates lay jewelled mounds of salad; agate, chrysoprase, topaz and garnet, leaves of carved jade which the firelight fretted with shadows, and atop each pile a thin Turkish crescent of gold and porcelain white. The pungent scent of chopped mint hid a less agreeable odour, rank and mousy. But none of Florence's faculties were very keen.

'It looks delicious,' said Florence, tucking in her napkin.

'I hope it tastes as good as it looks.'

Mrs. Jolly cut bread and butter and poured the tea, while Florence — oh, so terribly slowly, as it seemed to Mrs. Jolly — cut her salad across and across into refined mouthfuls. Then she balanced on her fork a morsel of this, a morsel of that.

Upstairs Belinda barked angrily.

'Oh, she must have got shut in. Shall I go and let her out?' said Florence, politely rising from her seat.

'I put her there on purpose,' said Mrs. Jolly, rather shortly. 'She's been naughty.'

'You're never going to leave her up there to bark all the time, surely? If she keeps barking . . . won't it be very annoying?'

'I'll let her out in a minute. Don't

bother about it. Do sit down and eat your supper — dear.' She threw in the last word with an effort.

Reluctantly, Florence sat down again — she did so hate any sharp intermittent noise; a dog barking, a door banging — and recommenced building up a forkful of food.

Mrs. Jolly's hands rattled among the tea-cups. She did not look up. Not even when she heard a harsh and terrible noise in Florence's throat. Not even when she heard her croak unrecognizably — 'I feel . . . I feel . . . ' But from the corner of her eye she saw Florence's tiny claws clutch at the tablecloth as she struggled to rise. The crockery slid towards her, as she pulled herself arduously upwards a few inches. Abruptly, she toppled over . . .

Mrs. Jolly quickly and methodically stacked everything back upon the tray and carried it out into the kitchen. Every particle of food was swept into the stove's red maw. There were to be no mistakes. The crockery was rinsed and dried, and replaced on the dresser. She worked with astonishing speed and accuracy, unflustered, as though it were part of a well-known routine to her. Yet she was surprised to hear herself breathing loudly and to find herself constantly glancing, half-unconsciously, at her wristwatch.

She marched back to the living-room. She was appalled to see Florence kneeling on the floor, clutching the chair with one hand, her waist with the other, bent over with an expression of agony on her grey face.

It gave Mrs. Jolly such a turn she almost screamed. As it was, for all her presence of mind, she stood stock still and stared at her. Florence, her loosened hair clinging in damp strands to her forehead, gazed back at her inarticulately, her glazed eyes full of desperate appeal. She looked like a stricken animal to Mrs. Jolly, whose heart overflowed with tenderness towards animals.

She mouthed voicelessly: *Wa-ter!*

'You poor little thing! You poor little thing!' said Mrs. Jolly, her face creased with pity as she picked her up — she weighed nothing at all, really it was hardly credible! — and carried her up to her bedroom. She laid her on the bed and covered her mechanically with the eiderdown. Mrs. Jolly felt quite helpless and lost in the conflict set up in her by the sudden influx of pity and self-reproach where she should be feeling power and triumph. It was terrible to see people suffer, worse still to know that you had caused that suffering. But that was a weak and sentimental outlook, and if you were weak and sentimental in this world you were a fool, and fools went to the wall — she knew that much.

Watching the woman on the bed breathing in shallow gasps, her blue lips shrunk back baring her teeth, in a false porcelain grin, she thought — Why, she's nothing but a hollow bone with the wind blowing through it — nothing to be afraid of there. Anyone with an ounce of guts would simply put a pillow over her face and that would be the end of it. It would be a kindness to put her out of her misery, for she was too far gone to recover (thank goodness!), even if she fetched the doctor to her, which she was hardly likely to do. The pulse beneath her firm touch fluttered wildly irregular. Dreadful she looked, blue and shrivelled as a dried pea. Slits of white showed between her eyelids. She was groaning horribly. But still Mrs. Jolly could not bring herself to act. She simply couldn't lay hands on her. It was against her instinct. She felt the same sort of revulsion if she had to kill so much as a spider. She couldn't bear it, it sickened her. She lacked strength of character, that was all there was to it; but she could not endure to see suffering. She could not endure to hear those frightening, piteous groans now. She had to get away. Florence began to retch painfully.

It was abominable; it was too disgusting; people should not have to die so cruelly. How could God allow such things? And how could decent human beings be expected to stand by and watch it? She for one could not.

Florence opened her eyes.

'Doctor!' she gasped. 'Very ill . . . '

'Yes, yes,' said Mrs. Jolly eagerly, in a loud voice. 'I'll go and get the doctor. I'll go and fetch him myself. Do you understand? I won't be long.'

'Hurry!' the voice begged.

She'd hurry all right. Anything to get away, to preserve her firmness of purpose intact, uncontaminated by the weakness of compassion.

Through the dull agony, Florence heard her in the next room, moving about, then going downstairs and shutting the front door behind her, then the slow starting of the car, warming the cold engine into a deep even hum (oh, hurry, hurry, hurry, urged Florence mindlessly), then the backing, the braking, the grinding and turning it in the right direction, till at long last the sound of it died into the distance.

Then the anguished waiting, while all the clocks ticked her life away second by second. And she did not return . . . she did not return . . .

Some feeble corner of Florence's exhausted brain counted the seconds into minutes . . . There, that must be five minutes . . . And another five for good measure . . . Quarter of an hour; ten minutes at the least . . . Why did she not come back? Where was the doctor? The problems were too great for her to deal with. She could no longer reason. She was scarcely more than a tortured consciousness. She was dying, she knew.

Some instinct of life prompted her to rouse herself, to rally her strength. Help: she must find help. She would not die alone like a dog in a ditch.

Somehow she rolled off the bed. She moved with the clumsy uncertainty of a drunkard. Her legs felt like stumps, numb. Bent into an arc, she dragged herself as far as the door ... leant trembling against the jamb ... presently advanced again, using in the process as much energy and determination as a soldier on the last lap of a speed march. The stairs swayed steeply down into a black abyss below. She negotiated them finally by sitting down and sliding from step to step ... Then her strength was exhausted. There was no air left in her lungs for her labouring heart to pump ... Once more she tried to stand, and stumbled over ... She crawled grimly in the direction of the telephone, and lunged out desperately for the receiver . . .

Far away, somewhere under the vast roaring seas that swept over her icily in ominous black waves, she could hear a bell ringing . . . a bell that she knew meant something . . . a bell that was trying to attract her attention . . . something good.

The bell ceased abruptly and a tiny marionette's voice said — in her head or a hundred miles away — 'Number, please.'

She summoned the last forces of life and with a wonderful sense of triumph she spoke distinctly into the mouthpiece:

'*Doctor!*' and then more faintly, as the wave engulfed her: '*Help!*' before she collapsed, pulling the telephone down on top of her.

The minute voice squeaked interrogatively half a dozen times from the black vulcanite receiver, and then all was still . . . The cottage was silent, so silent that one could hear the small incessant sounds that an old house makes at night: the sharp occasional exclamation of an ancient beam, the ivy tapping a finger idly on an upstairs window, the excited scuffle of a bird beneath the roof, the wind singing shrilly over an uneven floor, the clicking of the death-watch beetle in a worm-rotten panel . . .

6

The Uninvited

The mistake she made, Mrs. Jolly told herself as she drove desperately through the night, was in relying on a herb of which she had no experience. She had felt certain of finding aconite, if not in the garden, in the surrounding countryside. But time pressed, as the little fool seemed to be using her wits, and she could not afford to linger. Hemlock, she had seen growing in a ditch not far away as she drove about the country that afternoon, and she had trusted her herbal which had assured her that death was instantaneous. Something had gone wrong. That the woman was bound to die, she was sure. But how long must she wait? That was the question which made her eyes strain ahead into the darkness as she drove. For every moment was of the greatest importance now; and there was so much

94

to be done. She stroked her dog's rough fur, comforted by the response of its lively, wriggling, warm little body, and muttered to herself anxiously, computing. She had been gone nearly half an hour; long enough surely; as long as she could spare, anyway. Besides, it was not safe to drive around too long, she might be noticed and remembered — later.

But as she slowed down at the approach to her cottage, her headlamps picked out a dark figure moving against the hedge, and she pressed her foot down hard on the accelerator and shot past him. It would never do for anyone to see her drive up to the cottage at this time of night, far too risky. She made a rough circle and came back to the lane unobserved this time.

She slipped quickly through the front door and leaned back against it, listening to the deadly quiet, and breathing a heartfelt sigh of relief. With steady fingers she struck a match and lit the lamp on the table. She pulled off her hat and coat and glanced about her alertly. The heap on the floor attracted her eye at once.

She felt the blood rush up into her face at the sight. How had she got downstairs? And why? Was she — ? She bent over her with the lamp. What was that lying in the crook of her shoulder?

But before her mind could grasp the full significance of the woman's dead body on the floor by the window-seat, a sudden noise startled her so that she all but dropped the lamp, and for safety's sake put it back on the table. The doorbell! It sounded again and was followed almost at once by a double knock. Belinda barked angrily. Mrs. Jolly stood there thunderstruck, still holding the garments in her hand, like a ninny, with her frank blue eyes bolting from her head as though she was a mere country bumpkin who had seen a ghost.

Successive impulses drove her blood this way and that from second to second . . . Don't let them in . . . You must, because of the car, because of the light, because of Belinda . . . Run away . . . Set the place on fire with the lamp . . . They're knocking again. What can it be . . . ? You'll have to let them in . . .

looks funny not to . . . but hurry, hurry, hurry!

Suddenly she was galvanized into activity again. She tossed her hat and coat out of sight behind the curtain . . . bent down and replaced the receiver on the hook of the telephone . . . caught the body immodestly by the legs and dragged it swiftly upstairs . . . shoved it into the little bedroom and shut the door.

She ran back again downstairs, swearing inwardly, and tidying her hair as she came — and glanced hastily round to see that nothing was revealed that should be hid. Her breathing was still uneven when she opened the front door, though the outer darkness hid her flushed face.

A large black shape hid the greater part of the night sky from her.

'Yes?' she said uninvitingly.

The man said deeply:

'This *is* Ivy Cottage, isn't it?'

'It is.'

'I believe my services are required for someone here.' He advanced towards the threshold as he spoke, but still she barred the way. Drat the woman, keeping him out in the rain, he thought.

'I think there is some mistake,' she said evenly.

'I am the doctor,' he said. And added: 'They rang me up from the telephone exchange about ten minutes ago and said they thought someone at Ivy Cottage wanted a doctor.'

'Oh, you're the doctor!' exclaimed Mrs. Jolly, suddenly understanding. 'How stupid I am! Whatever must you think of me? Do come in, and I'll explain what happened.' She closed the front door, thinking rapidly.

She shifted the lamp rather to one side so that the light should not fall on her face, and pushed forward an arm-chair.

'Won't you sit down?'

'Hadn't I better see the patient first?'

'There isn't one,' said Mrs. Jolly. 'Or rather, I am the patient.'

'Ah!' He sounded relieved . . .

He drew a chair close to her. 'And what's the trouble?'

She turned her head a little away.

'To be quite candid, nothing at all. I

feel ashamed to have dragged you out on a wretched wet night like this for nothing.'

'But you did send for me?'

'Oh yes, I'm afraid so.'

'I mean, it was *you* who sent for me?'

'Oh yes. I live alone.'

'I see.' He glanced round him curiously. 'Well, since I *am* here, hadn't you better tell me what the trouble is?' he suggested reasonably.

'I felt dreadful. Everything went black all of a sudden. I suppose I must have fainted. I've never felt like that before and it frightened me. I got to the 'phone, but I didn't have time to look up your number or anything of that sort. Then I must have gone off. I don't remember anything else. But I'm quite all right now.'

'Mmmm!' said the doctor, pulling the lamp towards him and turning, up the wick. 'We'll have a little more light on the subject, if you don't mind.' He took her reluctant wrist between his fingers and watched her run her tongue over her dry lips. 'Mmmm!' he said again. 'Pulse quite strong and regular, but a little too

99

rapid. Sleeping well . . . ? Bowels regular?'

'I feel rather a fraud,' said Mrs. Jolly, with something of a laugh. 'I'm as strong as a horse really. I've never fainted in my life before.' She stooped and picked Belinda up, settling her on her knee, stroking her lovingly in order to calm herself. The dog's familiar presence gave her a feeling of security. Hardly listening to the doctor's words of advice, she pressed her flushed face against Belinda's hairy little body and murmured love-words into her pricked ears. She could have sworn she had heard a sound upstairs. If only that fool of a doctor would keep talking; or better still, go away. Belinda's heart beat faster than her own, she noticed, but Belinda had nothing to be afraid of.

There! There it was again! Four soft distinct steps. She could not help an involuntary glance at the doctor. He was sitting up with his head cocked at the same alert angle as the little Cairn's. It was enough to make a cat laugh.

'Did you hear anything?'

'Birds in the rafters,' she explained

casually. 'I know, I've lived in old houses before.'

'Would you like me to investigate?'

'Good heavens, no; I wouldn't waste your time, doctor. What do you anticipate — burglars?' she said, with a laugh.

'If you'll just slip off your blouse, I'll sound your heart before I go. And then, if you'll come down to the surgery tomorrow or the day after, between four and six-thirty, I'll give you a thorough examination.' She was certainly a cool customer, he thought. He was curious to know more about her and tried to pump her discreetly.

A floorboard creaked above. A second later there was a reverberating crash. Belinda quivered in her arms. She hoped it was not possible to discern in the lamplight how pale she had gone suddenly. She had felt the blood drain from her face. Without imagination as she was, she yet had a horrible vision of the dead woman appearing at the head of the stairs accusingly, like Banquo's ghost.

'Birds?' said the doctor sardonically.

She flushed. 'You'd never believe what a noise they can make. It is incredible.'

'Well, your nerves are all right, that's one thing,' he laughed. '*I* shouldn't be able to sleep of nights with all that thumping and scuffling going on, and I daresay my conscience is as clear as yours.'

'I daresay it is,' agreed Mrs. Jolly blandly, wondering how many people he had killed — in the course of his professional duties, of course: but still, killing was killing. She yawned tremendously and apologised with a smile.

He took the hint.

'You must be off to bed.'

'I must, indeed.'

'And I shall expect you tomorrow afternoon.'

'Yes, do,' she said sweetly. 'And I hope I'm forgiven for dragging you out on a fool's errand.' She held out her hand frankly, her ingenuous blue eyes meeting his almost for the first time. 'Goodnight, and thank you.'

'Goodnight, and *au revoir.*'

She nodded affably, nodded as she

listened to the car chugging into the distance, and then wiped the grin off her face abruptly. Too much time had been wasted, and before anything else was done she must go upstairs and find what had made that noise, whose steps she had heard moving softly across the floor. Common sense told her that it could not be the dead woman. Whatever it was, she had to face it. She was not without physical courage.

She picked up the lamp in one hand, the poker in the other, and advanced to the foot of the staircase. Then thoughtfully she put the lamp down again and drew from her pocket a slim torch. It occurred to her that if anyone was up there a lamp might be knocked from her hand and set the place on fire; a torch was safer.

She moved softly up the stairs, casting the wavering beam into first one shadowy corner and then another. There was a little clod of mud on the strip of coconut matting that ran between the two rooms, but whether it came from her own shoe or not she could not tell.

In Florence's room the round table that stood in the middle of the floor, as a rule, had fallen over on its side. Mrs. Jolly stood there with her hand on the door, staring at it, trying to understand its significance. The curtains flapped and crackled in the draught from the open door. The window was wide open. There was a long smear of mud on the painted sill.

Mrs. Jolly switched off her torch and stood in the dark by the open window, letting the fresh moist air blow in her face, and trying not to be afraid.

Someone had been there, no doubt about that. And there could be no reasonable doubt either that they had seen the body on the floor. Perhaps even now they were on their way to the police station. Perhaps the man who called himself a doctor had been a policeman in disguise, sent to distract her attention while they made a search upstairs. Perhaps they were returning with a warrant for her arrest at this very moment.

A thin red line of blood trickled down

her chin from the pressure of her teeth. *Don't be a fool! Pull yourself together, Vi!*

She groped for the lamp and lit it. Shut the window and pulled the curtains. Then turned her attention to the body on the floor, flexing a cold limb gently. There was no time to be lost!

Methodically she attended to all the gruesome details which lay before her. Now that the thing beneath her hands was no longer capable of experiencing sensation, she had no more fear of it. She had no respect for it, even as a creature that had once moved and breathed; she treated it as ruthlessly and unfeelingly as a sawdust dummy. If she thought about it at all, it had become merely a symbol of her own extraordinary cleverness and power. But she had no time for her thought to soar in speculation: what had to be done had to be done quickly, before rigor mortis rendered it impossible.

When the corpse had been stripped of every single article that had not been a living part of it, she fetched a quantity of newspaper and a length of sash-cord, with which she trussed the carcass — head between knees and heels against hams — into the smallest possible compass, and then wrapped it round and round in newspaper.

Only then did she dare seek her real objective. She pulled open the chest of drawers roughly, spilling the things out on the floor. There was the thin blue Savings Book she sought. She opened it eagerly: Florence had told her more than once that she had some eight hundred pounds saved up. 'Bloody little fool!' swore Mrs. Jolly, with unaccustomed violence, for there were barely two hundred pounds there. She could have cried with disappointment. Served her right, the little liar, that she was dead. If she had told the truth she might still be alive — it was too late now.

Mrs. Jolly got on with the job. She pulled the suitcases from under the bed and examined the contents carefully, as well as the articles on the floor, holding them up against the light, searching them for flaws and estimating their probable worth, while noting the identification marks. These last she unpicked carefully and collected in a scrap of paper, which she burnt in the stove later. It was not a very grand list. Two pairs of walking shoes, in fairly good condition; one pair of bedroom slippers, poor quality and badly worn; a pair of dressy afternoon shoes with high heels; three pairs of stockings, much mended, and one pair unworn; five handkerchiefs; a grubby pink-satin girdle; two vests and three pairs of pants; a green woollen cardigan suit; two silk blouses; a brown tweed skirt; a navy wool frock, and an overcoat that almost matched; three art-silk night-dresses; a blue felt hat; a green silk scarf; an imitation Jaeger dressing-gown, very shabby; a fur tie; brown suede gloves, and a brown leatherette bag. So much for the clothes. There were the usual odds and ends too that a woman collects about her; toilet things and little boxes of cream and powder, half-empty bottles of lavender water and Odo-ro-no, hair curlers and kirby-grips. There was also a small haul of semi-precious jewellery; a little ring with a pinkish ruby, a gold link-bracelet, a necklace of seed pearls, a little miniature brooch set in enamel and marquisate; no more than could be worn together unobtrusively, and which in fact the dead woman had always worn. They still seemed faintly warm to the touch, or perhaps Mrs. Jolly's hands were cold.

Then everything was carefully repacked in the boxes and carried out to the car, where she propped the suitcases against the back seat. Her own things she had packed in readiness earlier in the day, and stripped her bed and left the room prepared for her departure. It looked as though no one had been there. The other room must be made to look the same.

With gloves on her hands, she picked up the fallen table, emptied the flower vases, swept up every scrap of spilt powder and tiny ends of cotton, removed every tell-tale sign of habitation, and left the bed-linen piled neatly on the mattress. She stooped and with an effort lifted the clumsy newspaper package from the floor and staggered downstairs with it. It was heavy, cumbersome, not easy to carry, and she was glad she had not to take it far.

One last look round upstairs, closing all the windows, and extinguishing the lamp. Then, downstairs, and a careful scrutiny of the living-room, emptying betraying ashtrays, burning the oddments that remained in the kitchen larder, and when they were consumed, raking the last glowing coals out of the stove. She locked the kitchen windows and back door.

She put on her outdoor clothes. She glanced round once more, anxiously. Was there anything she had forgotten? She turned out the lamp and opened the front door, peering into the darkness, listening. Satisfied after a moment or two that all was well, she hurried to the car, tossed her handbag in at the window, and opened the luggage-shoe at the back of the car. The dog followed her anxiously, like a little black shadow.

She returned to the house, and came stumbling out in a minute with her grotesque parcel. She thrust it into the shoe, stuffing it well in, and then banged it shut and locked it. Then she locked the front door of the house, chucked the key meditatively into the air once or twice and then tossed it over her shoulder into an adjacent flower-bed . . . That was that.

She drew a deep breath and stared up at the sky. The moon had set and a few stars pricked slyly between the racing, torn clouds. There was a high wind now with a promise of further rain. She got into the car. As she turned at right angles to the village, she heard above the engine's purr the resonant note of the church clock striking one.

7

Mrs. Jolly Disposes of a Parcel

She drove along the twisted, rutted lanes. The headlights jolting on the hedgerows picked out leaves and twigs diamonded with past rain, and ran long golden fingers over the trunks of trees. Small animals scuttled to safety in the grass verge. Presently she turned the car northward, running it smoothly on the macadam that flowed like blue-black water beneath the glow of the lamps. Filled with the vitality of success, she was intensely aware of everything. She longed to release some of her excessive exhilaration with the luxury of speed, but she dared not risk a speed-trap even at that hour. Still, there was no traffic to speak of on the road and it was a little after three that she left the main road for one of the small roads that led to Wimbledon Common.

The Common was deserted and she drove slowly up and down looking for the sort of place she wanted: somewhere not too far from the road, affording a reasonable amount of cover, and at the same time remote from the tiresome intermittent street lamps.

It should have been so easy to find, theoretically, and yet either there was a parked car nearby or some other danger. Once or twice she got out of the car to investigate a likely spot. Once she came to a dark hollow thick with shrubs, only a few feet actually from the path but screened from it by a group of trees — the very place she was looking for — but as she slithered down the muddy bank into the dip, she felt herself falling, grabbed at a branch, felt her feet arrested by sudden impact with something softish and yielding, and heard to her startled ears a squeal of protest.

Two opaque but invisible monsters rose from the ground under her feet.

''Ere, what's going on?' inquired an injured male voice.

'Can't yer look where yer going? Some

people ... honestly!' came a cockney flute obbligato.

'You all right, ducks?'

'Not much! Trod all over me, 'e did. Gotta nawful bruise on me — ' (a giggle that was not unattractive) 'Oooh! go on Harry! I was only going to say me *shin*.'

Mrs. Jolly moved silently away and the grumbling duet faded from earshot. There was nothing about her that they could possibly recall and recognize later, and it occurred to her also that people who did their love-making out of doors might have good reason to desire secrecy and, in any case, would hardly be likely to publish the fact abroad. All the same, it was unfortunate; the situation would have been perfect.

She drove on. The next time she halted she snapped Belinda's leash on to her collar and took her too. Belinda's senses were more acute than hers and she would prevent her butting into some petting-party again. This time she stopped near a road and, when she got out, she dimmed the lights and left the engine running. She found nearby a piece of rough ground which, from the prevalence of the gorse springing up abundantly in thorny knots a few inches high, tore at her ankles, and spiky bushes that came above her shoulder, she guessed to be an unfrequented part. With her gloved hands she beat back the branches of one low-lying clump till there was a large enough cavity to hold and conceal the body.

She was just starting back to the car when she heard, faintly at first, but growing steadily louder and clearer, advancing footsteps. A ponderous, unmistakable tread. She waited, heart beating, for them to pass and die away. But they ceased abruptly in almost a deadline with her. He must be at the car. Why else should he have halted? A yellowish thread waved about, now long, now curling to a point of light, as the policeman cast his torch-beam here and there.

She marshalled her wits. The sooner she returned to her place the less reason would he have for undue inquisitiveness in regard to number-plates and license registrations.

She saluted him without looking at

him. 'Evening, Officer.' She opened the door and slid into the driving-seat as she spoke, grateful for the turned-down brim of her hat. She tugged at the leash and patted the seat beside her.

'Ah,' said the constable, 'I was just wondering what 'ad become of the owner. You never ought to leave the engine running, ma'am. Anyone could make off with it as easy as easy. Asking for trouble, it is.'

'I was just taking the doggy for a little run,' she explained. 'Thank you for standing by, Officer, though I don't think I was gone more than a minute.'

'There's a nice little dog!' said the policeman, patting Belinda's head impertinently. She snapped at the air saucily just after his fingers had passed caressingly over her muzzle. 'Proper little nipper, ain't she?' he said admiringly. 'Well, I'd best be getting along.'

'A lonely beat, Officer.'

'That's right, Miss. Wouldn't do to be afraid of the dark. 'Night, Miss.'

''Night, Officer.' The car shot past him. Of all the infernal bad luck! Really, nothing had gone smoothly for her that evening; she had constantly to pit herself against unforeseen circumstances. What was she to do now? Dared she look for another place? The point was, how big was his 'beat', and how long did it take to cover it? Suppose she stopped somewhere else and he or another came up, might it not look odd, even suspicious?

Now she was feeling tired. The hour was late for her and she had had nothing to eat for a long while. The excess of nervous energy with which she had been flooded was subsiding and giving place to a nervous lassitude. For two pins she would have fallen asleep over the wheel. But that damnable burden had to be disposed of.

She skidded up the Putney High Street. Rain made the wind-screen like a sheet of water and the road as sharply slippery as glass. Fragments of poetry and half-forgotten tunes came into her mind, and she drew consolation from them repeatedly under her breath, ' . . . his withered cheek and hair of grey seemed to have known a better day . . . a maid whom

116

there was none to praise and very few to love . . . they call her the lass with the delicate air . . . the lass of Richmond Hill.' Richmond Hill! With a sudden spin of the wheel she turned the car round. 'If at first you don't succeed, try, try, try again,' she continued with her childish maunderings. And why not, after all, try Richmond Park? Her spirits revived. The heavy rain was a good omen that would wash away footprints and tyre tracks.

On the empty by-roads that led to the Park she became aware of a pair of headlights behind, far-off, that kept a steady distance and never advanced to overtake her, though the roads were quite clear. It did not occur to her for some time that she was being followed, and when it did, she dodged down side-turnings to try and shake him off. She made sure she had before she entered the Park. But once on a solitary stretch of ground she drove more slowly, looking about her on this side and that.

A car flashed past. She thought nothing of it, till she saw it swerve across the road, blocking it from curb to curb, and a man standing out in the roadway with arm upraised. Even then her first thought was of a police trap rather than a holdup. There was no room to turn. She could not back out of this man-made cul-de-sac. And every split second she was drawing nearer. She was always at her best in an emergency and her wits did not fail her now, tired though she was. Since she could not retreat she must advance. And advance she did, stamping down on the accelerator and clenching her jaws. The man sprang out of the way of the juggernaut in the nick of time. She saw the herring-bone pattern of his coat quite plainly. The other car loomed across her bonnet. She pulled violently at the wheel — saw sky and earth make one strange chunky design — and the car lurched over the curb, bumping along the uneven turf and out of range.

Yes, but the event had given her a nasty shock, a shock that she could have withstood at the beginning of the evening, but which overcame her now and left her trembling.

She could no longer force her body to

obey her will. She was exhausted. She was too old for the strain that had been put upon her the last few hours, she thought self-pityingly. She damned the corpse that she carried with her, like the sinister albatross. In an hour or so it would be getting light and then it would be too late to do anything till the following night . . . Come what might, she must sleep. She was almost too weary to drive to the central London hotel and garage the car in the super-modern garage they provided, with a ramp that ran upwards like the tower of Babel and downwards like the circles in Dante's Inferno.

In the plush, air-conditioned, streamlined hotel even at that hour of the morning there was so much clatter and movement, so many lifts and corridors and buttons and lights, that she was quite dazed. Their slogan was 'Open all night.' It was like a railway station, with people arriving from the ends of the earth and setting off in the opposite direction the very next day, as like as not. People rarely spent more than forty-eight hours there. The staff never bothered to look at your face, for you were not likely to return, and if you did return you were not likely to be attended to by the same shift of servants.

Mrs. Jolly dropped her clothes on the floor and tumbled on to the bed. She fell asleep heavily and instantly.

She awoke about eleven and ate an enormous breakfast, admiring her own relish. Belinda sat on the bed beside her, being petted and fed with tit-bits from her tray. She stretched her limbs till they cracked, grunting with delight, and tickled the Cairn's stomach. It was a fine day. A pale sun gilded the dusty streets with dancing motes and overhead small clouds reclined languidly in a sky thinly washed with blue. It was good to be alive on such a day, and she felt more intensely alive than usual because of her constant awareness of Florence dead. She was filled with an agreeable sense of her own superiority. Of course the little fool had lied to her. She had expected that to a certain extent, for people always lied about money. But she had not dreamed of an exaggeration to the tune of six hundred pounds.

Yet after all two hundred pounds odd was not to be sneezed at for less than a fortnight's work, and most of it sheer profit at that. Mrs. Jolly kept the most meticulous accounts and she knew to the last farthing what she had spent on Florence, from the first fivepence she had spent on coffee in the station buffet to the last gallon of petrol used for the disposal of her carcass. She expected to get her money back on the clothing and trinkets alone. Yes, two hundred pounds was not bad, and she had no right to grumble.

She sprang out of bed. She had a busy day ahead of her. The first thing she did was to take from her bag one of the papers she had caused Florence to sign among the sheaf of forms a day or two before her death. This was a withdrawal form, and with the help of the Savings Book Mrs. Jolly filled in the necessary details to draw out all the money and close the account. To be collected from the Liverpool Post Office. Then she placed them together in an envelope and addressed it. Next, she scrawled something on a sheet of hotel notepaper, stuck it in an envelope and addressed it to Miss F. Brown, Grand Hotel, Northern Road, Liverpool. The letter she dropped in the hotel box. The Savings Book she had registered at a post office, where she also bought a sheet of paper and a stamped envelope. Next she went into the typewriter department of a big store and tested one of the machines by writing an address on the just-purchased envelope: Miss F. Brown, Grand Hotel, etc. Yes, the same address as before, and she hoped that two letters would suffice for her purpose. She made some excuse to the inattentive assistant and drifted out again.

Tucking Belinda under her arm, she jumped on a bus for Aldgate, which would take her within walking distance of Browne, Hoggers & Whitely, the firm where Florence had worked for nearly twenty years. Interesting facts she had revealed about it; they made some very curious and useful articles.

She passed a pillar-box and dropped in the last letter.

In the dim front room where travellers were received and samples displayed,

Mrs. Jolly stared about her at the unusual assortment of objects: an antique chased telescope, prisms, filters, and cases wherein glass eyes reposed delicately on black velvet.

'I understand you make contact lenses,' she said to the pale young man inclining before her.

He admitted it.

'I would like a pair.'

He half-smiled. They were a wholesale firm, he explained, they had no retail trade.

'Oh dear!' She sucked in her lip girlishly. Might she explain the situation to him? She was sure he could help her. The fact was she was an actress, a film actress, and she had been offered such a part: in a film about the American Deep South, she was wanted to play the part of a black woman. Perfect! A little cameo of acting. She cast down her eyes modestly. They seemed to think only she could play the part. And she would simply adore to do it. She had had the test. Technicolor, it was. And there lay the snag. She opened her eyes wide, appealingly. Her eyes were

123

blue. Wasn't it absurd!

The young man gazed at her blankly.

You see, people were so particular about the accuracy of those little details. Blue eyes would not do. Whoever heard of a black woman with blue eyes! She had been in despair, till a friend of hers had told her of a similar case, where tinted contact lenses had been used with the happiest results. And if the kind young man would come to her rescue — she did not require special sight, only that they should make her eyes appear brown — she promised faithfully, faithfully, never to mention it to a living soul. She could promise that truthfully enough, she thought ironically.

Because she was determined to have them, she got them. The young man was rather amused, though she was hardly his idea of an actress — such a sensible-looking woman; more like a farmer's wife than anything else, in his opinion. He fitted her up with a pair of sample lenses that were not too uncomfortable. And he tinted the iris-part brown with a glass dye, while she waited. And he showed her how to fit them between the lids and how to remove them after a few hours' wear with a little suction cup.

Her delight seemed out of all proportion to the importance of the things; but theatrical folk, he knew, were ultra-excitable. *Uncle Tom's Cabin*, she told him, was the name of the film and she promised him a seat at the premiere.

When she arrived back at the hotel she ordered a meal. And when she had eaten it, collected her luggage, paid her bill and went round to the garage to fetch her car. With a sigh of thankfulness she drove through the drab environs of London in the gathering dusk.

She resisted the gnawing impulse to look in the luggage-shoe to see whether the body was still there. It must be, because she had locked it in herself. She drove northward to Epping Forest. Presently she stopped the car and walked, awed in spite of herself, through the long silent aisles that arched darkly overhead like the fretted roof of some cathedral.

She left her gruesome parcel beneath a clump of bushes and covered the disturbed earth with broken fronds of bracken and dead leaves. It was very still. She raised her hand in a jaunty salute. 'Goodbye, Miss Brown. Rest in peace!'

8

Should Auld Acquaintance Be Forgot...

While she waited for the Liverpool General Post Office to inform her that the money was there, Mrs. Jolly occupied herself by looking for a suitable car to part-exchange for her own. It was a necessary caution to cast off her tracks behind her. You never could tell what people might memorize about a car — men seemed to notice the least peculiarity about a car that differentiated it from the million others like it. So she wanted to get rid of it as soon as possible.

She found a small garage eventually in an obscure side street, and in it an almost new Morris, which was just what she wanted. She spent a day or two bargaining with the proprietor most agreeably, and they finally settled on a price that in some marvellous way seemed to satisfy them both.

Practically all the rest of the time, she spent writing for hours on end in a cheap exercise book. And what she wrote was simply the same two words over and over again: *Florence Brown*. It should have been easy enough to copy the real Florence Brown's handwriting: there was nothing very unusual about it, no pronounced characteristics; it was the rather slovenly copperplate type of the semi-educated clerk. The difficulty for Mrs. Jolly lay in subduing her own characteristic, upright, running script, written with a thick nib. She could, by drawing a replica of the signature slowly and carefully, produce an adequate copy, a copy good enough to pass a cursory glance, but that would not do. She would be required to sign the form again at the Post Office, on the same paper that earned the original signature. It would not do for her laboriously to copy it as she would a drawing, she must be able to make a rapid and convincing reproduction. And this was not going to be so easy. To increase her nervousness there would be the added inconvenience of not writing comfortably at a desk or table, but standing, bent awkwardly over a counter, with people pushing against one, writing on a rough scrap of paper with a miserable apology for a pen.

It made her blood run cold to think of such an ordeal, and she thanked her stars for the wisdom that had made her dispatch those letters in Florence's name from London to the hotel in Liverpool. She patted the bag she carried them in with satisfaction. The anticipation of all possible pitfalls was the criminal's best safeguard. Overconfidence and want of imagination were the cause of most crimes failing, she thought, and commended herself for her own astuteness.

The day she went to collect the money, she spent a long time dressing herself suitably. She discarded her heather-mixture wool stockings and brogues in favour of silk stockings and high-heeled shoes. She chose a drab raincoat as the most unnoticeable outer garment one could wear. Instead of her usual plain felt, she wore a woollen turban, under which was concealed every scrap of hair. That already altered her appearance a lot, making her face seem much fuller and heavier. With a little tube of mascara she darkened her white eyebrows and a wisp of hair in front, which she frizzed up into a fringe on her forehead. Last of all, she inserted the brown glass shells under her eyelids so that they fitted closely to her eyeballs. Round her right index finger she wound a thick bandage and fastened it with a safety-pin, over which she pulled a loose finger-stall. She wore a glove on her left hand, and carried the other.

On the landing she nearly ran into a tall, well-built, bold-faced looking woman in her forties. And when she realised it was herself reflected in a wall-mirror, she gave a delighted smile. The unaccustomed high heels made quite a difference to her height and build, altering even her posture. Her face looked altogether cruder now that it was not framed in soft white hair. And the dark, expressionless stare of her new eyes made her glance bolder. If she did not recognize herself, it was unlikely that anyone else would know her.

The bored girl behind the grille pushed the form towards her.

'Sign, please.'

She moved along to a sort of shelf, partitioned off into little booths containing telegraph forms and battered pens. She sucked her cheeks in tightly between her teeth, and wrote. She contrived, as she blotted it, to smudge it slightly. The result, she considered, was not too bad.

She slid it across to the counter, hopefully.

The girl looked at it critically, a frown puckering her pale brows.

Mrs. Jolly said hastily, with deceptive lightness:

'I'm afraid it's not too good, but I can't hold the pen properly with my finger.'

She held it up to be observed. The girl observed it, sullen, unsmiling. 'And your pen didn't improve matters,' continued Mrs. Jolly brightly. 'However, I am who I am.' She drew carelessly from her bag a couple of letters, or rather, envelopes ripped open indifferently, addressed to Miss F. Brown.

The blonde beauty flicked an eyelid at

them, sniffed, but condescendingly stamped the form, and opened the drawer behind her.

'Tens?' she asked frigidly.

Mrs. Jolly shook her head.

'All ones, please.'

The girl dampened her finger genteelly on the sponge and thumbed them methodically, counting beneath her breath. A heartbeat for every note, thought Mrs. Jolly standing there in agony, calmly smiling. People edged against her impatiently, and moved on, seeing it was to be a lengthy business. It would have been nice to make a joke to relieve the unbearable tension she felt, but there was no one to whom she could make it, and she did not dare to interrupt the silent counting.

The restlessness caused by her anxiety became uncontrollable, and she moved away, pacing a few steps this way and that. At that moment a high-pitched feminine voice behind her exclaimed:

'Why, Violet! This *is* a surprise! I'd never thought to have seen you here.'

Mrs. Jolly turned involuntarily to see who was speaking and found at her elbow a small bleached woman with shrewd eyes in a lively little monkey face.

'Why, how you've altered!' she said with a look of astonishment. 'I'd never have known you. And there's a silly thing to say,' she laughed, 'because I recognized you at once. But you know what I mean. Good heavens! I said to myself, if it isn't Violet Russell . . . after all these years. Well, I never!'

'I'm afraid you've made a mistake,' said Mrs. Jolly pleasantly.

'Get on!' the little woman adjured her good-naturedly. 'And I suppose you've never seen little Kitty Weston before, either?'

'I have not that pleasure. My name is Brown.'

Kitty Weston flashed a pillar-box smile at her.

'Brown it may be now, I'm not saying anything about that; Brown's a name as good as another, and easy to remember, isn't it? That's none of my business. I don't mind telling you that I've got another name myself since Daddy hopped it with his latest soulmate . . . ' She winked. 'But don't tell me your name wasn't Russell in the good old days down at Christbourne. I knew your voice as soon as I heard it.'

'My name is Brown,' Mrs. Jolly repeated clearly, and added with chilly firmness: 'I'm afraid you're confusing me with someone else. Excuse me, please.'

'Pardon me,' murmured the little woman, unabashed. 'It must have been two other guys.'

'Two hundred and eleven pounds — ' said the girl, pushing them across with two half-crowns, in the same impassive manner with which she would have sold a two-shilling postal order or a dozen penny stamps, ' — and five shillings. Thank you.'

'Thank *you*,' said Mrs. Jolly civilly, taking the money with hands that shook imperceptibly and, moving into a quiet corner, she began to count. Her impulse was to get the hell out of there as fast as she could. She did not obey it, partly because it was only normal to count such a large sum and she must still act as normally as possible — she was not yet beyond danger; and partly because she wished to observe from the corner of her eye what had become of that sickening little busybody — Mrs. Weston, as she called herself.

Mrs. Weston bought her stamp, or whatever it was, and went . . . Seventy-six, seventy-seven, seventy-eight, seventy-nine — Mrs. Jolly continued mechanically. It took a long time to count two hundred and eleven pounds, but Mrs. Jolly would gladly have gone on twice as long. She found it a pleasure. She stuffed the notes lovingly into her bag.

Now it was all completed. She felt warm and bubbly in her chest with the sense of freedom and wealth and a tricky job successfully accomplished. She was walking on air, despite her uncomfortable shoes.

Therefore it jolted her nastily when a hand on her arm jerked her to a standstill and she looked down to see that Mrs. Weston again, smiling up at her.

'I say, I really am sorry I spoke out of turn just now, old girl. But I wasn't to know, was I? Getting a bit slow in the uptake in me old age. Annie Domini, that's me!'

'I don't know what you're talking about, madam. I've already told you twice that you're mistaken. Will you please go away.'

The smile faded from her monkey face. 'A joke's a joke,' she said huffily. 'What's the gag, eh?'

'Listen! If you don't stop pestering me,' said Mrs. Jolly sharply, 'I shall call a policeman.' She pulled her arm away and walked on decisively.

'Here, here, here!' cried the little woman. 'What's the big idea? There's no need to talk to me like that. If you don't want to know me, that's O.K. by little Kitty. But don't kid yourself I don't know you, old girl. I didn't live next door to you for nearly ten years for nothing. I wouldn't forget that signet ring on your little finger, for one thing.' With which Parthian shot, she turned and walked briskly in the opposite direction.

Mrs. Jolly groaned inwardly, hesitated, and then turned in her tracks and started after her.

'Sorry, Kitty,' she said gently. 'That wasn't very nice of me, was it? Will you give me the chance to explain?'

'You needn't trouble yourself.'

'Now who's being unkind?' said Mrs. Jolly reproachfully.

'All right, you old bitch,' said Mrs. Weston, suddenly mollified. 'You always were a bit of a snob, I remember.'

'Let's go and have a drink and talk over old times,' said Mrs. Jolly.

Mrs. Weston cast her an admiring glance.

'You *are* going it, aren't you? Drinking! Well, we can't get a drink at this hour, worse luck; the pubs aren't open yet. But they say tea isn't bad. Ever tried it . . . ?'

★   ★   ★

'Yes, you have altered,' murmured Mrs. Weston, over the café table, 'and for the better, too. I can't think what the difference is, but you look younger somehow than you used to then. It's having a bit of a gay time, I suppose,' she said archly. 'Well, I'm glad to hear it.

Daddy and I used to feel ever so sorry for you, stuck there and never seeing any life. But I said to him when your old man died: 'If that girl's got any gumption it'll come out now, you'll see.' And I was right, wasn't I? So Brown's the name now, is it? Mrs., I take it?'

'You may take it or leave it alone,' said the other with a jovial laugh.

'What's he like?' said Mrs. Weston curiously.

What sort of reply was one supposed to make to a remark of that kind? Mrs. Jolly hurriedly drank some tea to gain time.

'What a question!' she laughed.

'Is he here with you?'

Mrs. Jolly nodded. She never had cared for the game of questions and answers.

'Are you living in Liverpool, now?'

'Oh no. Are you?'

'God forbid! I'm just up here for a few days' holiday with my friend. He had to make a business-trip. You know. Tell you what, we ought to make a little foursome some evening. This hole's as dull as ditchwater. Nothing to do but go off to bed.'

Mrs. Jolly laughed.

'Well, I'm not as young as I was, dear,' said Mrs. Weston seriously. 'And Len's awfully sweet, but he's not exactly a glamour boy ... How about having dinner with us tomorrow evening, if you're free?'

'I'd love to,' said Mrs. Jolly. 'Only, we're sailing for the States day after tomorrow.'

'Lucky girl!' observed Mrs. Weston, thinking she had certainly become uncannily elusive. And she was still puzzled to lay a finger on what exactly made Vi look so different from the old days. 'Hence the money!'

'What? Oh, the money. Yes. Quick eyes you've got, haven't you, Kitty? And you noticed my ring, too. You ought to be a detective ... Here, my bill, please, waitress!'

Something of uneasiness in the other's manner must have communicated itself insensibly to Kitty Weston, and in the strange way that the human mind builds up its impressions at random from a multitude of thoughts received, so the words ' ... quick eyes ... to be a detective' combined in Mrs. Weston's brain and caused her to look at Mrs. Jolly as she turned to call the waitress. The shock that glance produced was like a physical blow.

Now she knew what it was that had puzzled her. Violet's eyes had changed from blue to brown. Odd enough in itself. But in that moment of wild shock, when she realized it, Kitty Weston had seen the light shining unmistakably on a glass contour.

Her little monkey face could be quite expressionless when she chose, and she had the feminine ability of chattering lightly while the world swung upside down.

She did not understand why Violet should want to pretend her eyes were brown; but it seemed to her that one did not go in for such a troublesome disguise unless it was for some very good reason. And by 'very good reason' Mrs. Weston acknowledged to herself that what she really meant was 'very bad reason.' Her usual brashness deserted her. She was too cowardly to tell Vi outright and ask her what it meant. She was frightened.

Lennie would tell her not to be a silly goose. Perhaps she had already been silly in forcing Vi to acknowledge her in the first place, when she so obviously didn't want to be recognized. Now all she wanted was to get away from her.

And as Mrs. Jolly nursed the same ambition it proved fairly easy.

But: 'What did you say your name was now?' said Mrs. Jolly.

'I didn't. No names, no pack-drill, as the lads used to say.' Mrs. Weston was being cautious now. 'Keeps himself to himself, Len does. Nervous, you know.'

'Oh, he's married, is he?' said Mrs. Jolly understandingly.

'Aren't they all, dear,' sighed Mrs. Weston. 'Well, it has been lovely to see you again.'

'Hasn't it!'

She stood up.

'See you again sometime.'

Mrs. Jolly waved affably and smiled.

'Not if I see you first, sweetheart,' she said to herself.

With the money actually in her hands, providing so easy an escape in any direction that suited her fancy, she could not take too seriously the unfortunate coincidence of running into Kitty Weston. She was the last person to want to cause trouble.

Living as she was with a married man, they would both shun anything like notoriety.

But in bed that night her outlook changed, her thoughts ran in a minor fugue. Would she not have been wiser to have persisted in the denial of her identity, even after it had been proved by the ring? There must be other people in the world with bloodstone signet-rings in old-fashioned settings. She could have brazened it out. Or, having yielded on that point, should she not have made certain that she would run no risk of Kitty getting suspicious later on, by stopping her mouth once and for all? It would have been a simple matter to get rid of her. All she had to do was to drive her out into the suburbs somewhere, knock her on the head with a spanner and throw her into some pond or river. Even if the corpse was discovered after and listed as murder, there was no chance of it being linked up with her, for there were no threads connecting them. No one knew they had ever met before, it was not likely that anyone would remember seeing them together, they were both strangers up there, and best of all there was no way in which she benefited by the woman's death.

Motiveless crimes were almost always unsolvable.

A pity she had not thought of it at the time, she thought, pressing her hot forehead against the pillow; the time for such a thing was past. The risks were multiplied if she tried to get hold of her again. And meanwhile Kitty might even have mentioned meeting her, in the foolish inconsequential way women do, to the man she was living with, Len whoever he was.

If Mrs. Jolly had been able to hear the conversation between Len and Kitty a few streets away, lying in the dark in their plump twin beds, she might have felt too agitated to drop off into a doze as quickly as she did.

Kitty began her story as entrancingly as Scheherazade, by saying: 'Len, I've been a fool.' But she had got so mad when the old girl wouldn't own up that she knew her, she explained, that she had just gone on and on till she'd been forced to admit it. Quite different, she was, and it seemed amazing to Kitty, looking back on it, that she had been able to recognize her. 'All this money she'd got, too. I watched her counting it. Hundreds of pounds, I should think.' And then these glasses — did Len know anything about them? You wore them against your eyes, so they didn't show, instead of on your nose like ordinary spectacles. They were the latest thing.

But, brown! Didn't Len think that was funny?

Len thought he had heard of funnier things than that.

He was an old meanie, then. Oooh, what a turn it had given her. It made her go goosey all over to think of it.

'Feel!' she commanded.

Len obligingly felt. Like satin, he said. Like ivory, he said. Not like any goose

144

he'd ever met — not even like a gooseberry.

He was an old silly. Honestly, didn't he think it funny, taking everything together? She quite saw that one might have to wear dark brown glass for some special eye affliction — it was clever of Len to have thought of that — and one might not want to meet an old friend again, and one might be off to the States on a ship that wasn't sailing; but surely when one did all these things at the same time there was some reason for other people to get suspicious.

Had she ever told Len that when she was living with Sid —

'Oh, don't let's go back to when you were living with Sid,' protested Leonard. 'Muck-raking!'

'Jealous!' she said, and poked him sharply with her elbow. 'I don't want to talk about Sid. I only want to tell you that when this girl lived next door, her cat died — '

'Oh, Kitty, for God's sake! Aren't we going to get any sleep tonight? Suppose her cat died. What of it? Suppose she's robbed a bank. What of it? Who cares? What's it to do with us?'

'Suppose it was worse than robbing a bank?'

Well, supposing it was. What did she want to do about it?

'I only wondered whether I ought to tell the police what I know,' she said meekly.

'Good God Almighty!' He sat bolt upright in bed, shocked. 'The police! And have them round here asking all about us! You must be barmy, chuck! Here! You didn't tell her my name, did you?'

Men were all alike, thought Kitty wearily, as she reassured him. Thinking only of their own skins. If his precious wife and kids found out, it would be the end of the world.

'If you want my advice,' said Len heavily, 'you'll turn over and go to sleep, my girl, and forget all about it when you wake up tomorrow. You don't need to run into trouble in this life; the difficulty is to keep out of it.'

Maybe he was right, thought Kitty. He was no fool. And after all, they might only laugh in her face at the police station, for what did all she had to tell them amount to when you looked into it? She had no proof of anything. A cat had died in funny circumstances a few years ago. A friend had changed her identity. Len was right, there could be plenty of reasons for it.

'Len!' she called gently, and touched his shoulder.

'Elsie,' he muttered in his sleep, and flung out an arm vaguely.

'Silly old fool!' thought Kitty, angrily gritting her teeth; and changed her mind again . . .

The awesome inconsequence of truth. A man muttering the name of his wife in his sleep spun the first gossamer thread of a web stronger than steel.

PART TWO

THE EVOLUTION OF A MURDERESS

1

Prelude to Murder

The real name of the woman who called herself Mrs. Jolly was Violet Russell. At least, it was in the days when she lived with her father in a small villa, next door to Mrs. Weston. That was after Mrs. Russell died and they left Malvern where they were living then. They decided on Christbourne, a gaunt new settlement which was just coming into being, partly because the doctor advised the Bournemouth climate for the Colonel's health.

The Colonel was a fine example of a cracked pitcher. He had been forced to retire in his early fifties on account of his poor health. 'Life in India ruins a fellow's constitution!' Quite. Everyone knew that. But life in Malvern on the pension of an officer in the Indian Army ruined a fellow's temper and, worse still, the lives of his wife and child into the bargain.

Mrs. Russell was credited with having been a beauty in her day, and was still a fine-looking woman. Seeing them together it was hard to imagine that this handsome woman walked at the end of a string held by her husband, a wizened little man, thin as a chip, a head shorter than she was, with a face as sharp as a profile on an old Roman coin.

Violet was their only child. A good girl. A good daughter. In those days, before the last war, it rarely occurred to daughters to be anything else. To rebel, in the majority of cases, required too much passionate purpose: passion they may have had, those young ladies, it was the purpose they so often lacked. Besides, Violet adored her mother. And in her puritanical way, Mrs. Russell loved her daughter, but not perhaps as much as she loved her husband, whom she feared so and towards whom, as she well knew, her first duty lay. She always upheld her husband against her daughter, as it seemed to her a good wife should. But once the Colonel was out of the house — goodness knows how he passed the time!

— and the two of them were left alone together, things were quite different. They relaxed. They shared all manner of absurd little secrets. But Mrs. Russell's lovely brown eyes seemed always large with unshed tears, and she acquired a strange little habit of glancing quickly over her shoulder with a nervous placating smile. It gave Violet a pang to see.

As soon as she became old enough not to identify herself with her mother's emotions, she no longer feared her father, but she learned slowly and shamefully to loathe him.

Violet grew up belatedly; having no encouragement to develop, she remained dependent and childlike, apparently content to be spoon-fed. She was a nice-looking girl, with her mother's dark hair and fresh complexion and her father's firm profile and bright blue eyes. She was taught to be polite, but not how to attract; she was taught to be a lady, but not to be a woman; she was told what was good form in matters of dress, but not that clothes were meant to adorn and allure; she knew that the greatest thing that could happen to her was if some young man asked her to be the mother of his children, but no one explained how she was to encourage that achievement.

Yet in spite of all these disadvantages she had her romance. Jacko — Jack Durrant — was the kind of young man old ladies love, good-looking but not conceited, thoughtful but not effeminate, and always so well-mannered. Of course he had no money.

Was that a point to be considered? Not when one loved, decided Violet, who was tasting for the first time the intoxicating glory of being noticed. Besides, she knew that she had quite a respectable little sum (only father never would tell her exactly how much) left in trust for her by her grandfather till she should marry or else attain the shocking and unmarriageable age of thirty-five.

It was quite understood that Jacko escorted her everywhere.

They made a sweet couple, people said. Yes, indeed. And it was plain as the nose on your face that they were madly in love. In other words, they got on pretty well together. Kissing gave Violet a secret sense of shame — shame proportionate to the pleasure she enjoyed. She no longer believed kissing gave one a baby — that was something else, to do with the navel — but she had a shrewd, horrible idea that making love to someone you weren't married to sent you mad and blind.

One delicious evening, with the distant elms making a lace fan against the pale green sky, in which stars, liquid as tears, dropped slowly from branch to branch, Jacko mumbled some gauche phrase which served as a proposal.

That was probably Violet's happiest hour. He was to ask the Colonel's permission the next day. Violet hardly closed her eyes all night — from excitement, not because she doubted the result of the interview. She was sure her father would be glad to be rid of her, and her mother would be proud.

It did not turn out like that at all. Colonel Russell was coldly insulting, as he knew so well how to be. Mr. Durrant was no better than a penniless adventurer and deserved to be horse-whipped for his impertinence. Jacko was moved to speech. The Colonel, exciting himself to fury, had a heart-attack. Jacko left the house white to the lips. In a long letter to Violet he expressed fully all his rage and disgust, reiterating some of the phrases several times and ending with a declaration of his undying love for her. She read the last bit again, crying all the while. She could hardly believe her father could be so cruel.

'But I love him,' she wailed. As though that were reason enough to marry.

'He isn't suitable,' they told her patiently. 'When it is time for you to marry, your mother and I will choose someone suitable for you.'

That wasn't the idea at all. Couldn't they understand, she and Jacko loved one another madly. With permission or without it they would marry.

A vein throbbed in the Colonel's narrow temples, and he smiled icily.

'I think not.'

The point being that if she married without his consent she lost her inheritance; and the Colonel was enough of a character reader, enough of a man of the world to know that Durrant — even if he genuinely wanted her — would never take her without her money. And while he lived he would be damned (he explained this carefully to his wife) if he would drop more than a hundred a year off his own income in order to feather someone else's nest. Mrs. Russell said timidly that if they no longer had Violet to feed and dress surely they would not be so badly off.

'Try not to be a fool, Bella,' he said wearily. 'It doesn't cost anything like that to keep the girl. Besides, she helps in the house.'

'I want Vi to be happy,' whispered Mrs. Russell.

'And is marriage going to make her happy?' demanded the Colonel fiercely. 'Are you happy?'

'Oh, Frankie!' said Mrs. Russell, and her eyes filled with tears.

As far as she was concerned, the matter was now closed. Once the Colonel had made up his mind on a subject there was an end to discussion.

But Violet was not so easily satisfied, and no wonder, since it was her life they were disarranging so calmly. It was left to Mrs. Russell to reason her into a better frame of mind, without of course mentioning the basic cause of the trust money. The line she always took was that the Colonel in his amazing wisdom did not consider Durrant a suitable husband, and in this he was guided by no other consideration than love for his daughter and her ultimate good.

'Is my girlie so anxious to leave her nest?' she would ask in tender persuasion.

And Violet would stammer wistfully that if she had a home of her own Mummy could come and stay with her from time to time and get away from her father's endless tyranny.

And then sometimes Mrs. Russell would cry and say how bitter it was that her only child wanted to leave her, didn't mind a bit leaving her alone to bear everything, and yet she pretended to love her. It was cruel. She, who had given up her whole life to her daughter, received only this in return, that her one thought was to get away as soon as she could. It was enough to break one's heart! And so on and so forth.

'You got married,' accused Violet. 'Why shouldn't I have my chance? Can you blame me for wanting to get away from this place?'

'Aren't you happy, dear?' said her mother in amazement.

'Happy!' echoed Vi. She wasn't happy, but she hadn't known it till now.

But none of these scenes developed conclusively. She wrote to Jacko regularly, and they met whenever they could, at other people's houses where they had scarcely time to talk, or at the public library, standing side by side, pulling books nervously from the shelves, as they talked in whispers.

Harder to bear than her father's cruelty and her mother's plaintiveness, she found Jacko's inability to sweep her away in a romantic elopement. He explained to her, shamefaced, that he did not earn enough, not nearly enough to marry on.

'I don't mind being poor,' she cried.

It would not be fair to expect it of her.

'I'll wait,' she said gallantly. 'I don't mind how long.'

It would not be fair to expect it of her.

Jacko's was not a strong character, luckily for the Colonel. Encountering resistance, he yielded. He had his little accomplishments; and there would be other girls with a little money of their own; it was not as if he was in any hurry to get married. It was so different for a man; a bachelor had the best of it.

However, he was, he told himself, enough of a gentleman to leave her free for the attention of other suitors. He tactfully withdrew. The other suitors remained nonexistent.

Well, that was her chance, and she muffed it. She did not know how to hold him, and it was doubtful if he would have been much use to her if she had managed to bring it off, for at that time her character was too weak and undeveloped to rule him and he needed to be ruled.

So her small secret romance turned sour and sickened her. She dropped her rather prolonged girlhood and entered the flatter easier routine of the unmarried woman. She was always Miss Russell now. She became useful at church bazaars, and she learnt how to prattle agreeably to elderly ladies or chaff the boringly gallant old men at social teas. She lived dully on the surface of life, understanding nothing at all of the complicated social and economic structure which cracked and quivered from time to time but miraculously upheld her world.

She had some idea that when she was thirty-five and came into her little bit of money she would go away, see something of the world, perhaps; in any case, she would *do* something, she would not let it moulder away with her uneventful days.

But when the hour came to claim it, it was no longer there. Her father, very upright, very soldierly, tried to make her grasp what had happened. But investments were beyond her, she had never been any use with figures; percentages and her father's sternness — as though she were somehow to blame for what had happened — frightened her. One point

161

was clear from the interview, the money was gone.

His only defence was to try and explain the intricate system of speculation which had eaten it up. She could not follow it and did not attempt to. She pursued her attack; why had he not been faithful to his trust?

Mrs. Russell, coming into his den at that moment, said: 'You mustn't be angry, dearie. If Grandpa had left the money to me I should have given it to your father. You can't call it stealing when it's from your daughter. It was a misfortune, and Daddy's very sorry.'

'Shut up!' roared Colonel Russell. But it was too late. Violet had never thought of it as stealing. Once her mother had spread the word before her it seemed self-evident.

Now was the moment for vengeance, now she would see her father crumple and cringe. She could hardly contain her fury. It was impossible to deal with the matter there and then, she needed time to think it over and decide what was to be done. In hesitation she was lost.

She never was able to take any decisive action, as it happened, for before she reached any conclusion her mother fell desperately ill. Mrs. Russell realised she was dying before her daughter did.

The Colonel knelt by her bed sobbing.

Mrs. Russell's bloodless hand stroked his grizzled head languidly.

'Don't mind, Frankie,' she sighed between her puckered lips. With an effort she rolled her eyes round to the other side where stood her daughter. 'Look after him, Vi.' Her gaze was urgent, command-ing, appealing.

A death-bed's promise was not to be broken, Violet knew. Besides, after the death of her mother her own feelings underwent a change. For once in a way she and her father clung together. She was strangely softened by his grief. She saw him suddenly as pathetic, old — he had aged considerably after his wife's death — and helpless. They were both badly cut up. They were alone in the world, they had to stick by one another now. 'I never thought she'd go first,' he kept saying pitifully.

They moved away, right away; a change of scene, the doctor advised. Christbourne was bleak after Malvern. They rented a small unfurnished box of a villa at the beginning of an unmade road; the first of a row of crude little houses. There were no near neighbours. Christbourne was scarcely more than a few shops. It all seemed very dull and bare and flat.

Father subsided into petty invalidism. It was not easy to keep him contented. He grumbled constantly about everything, the climate, the Government, the trades people, the income tax, the type of people who were coming to live in the new houses in their road — not at all what he had been accustomed to. Most of this passed over Miss Russell's head, she had learnt not to listen. She had plenty to do now, unlike in the old days, for although the house was small and their wants few, she had to attend to everything herself.

In the summer there was always a violent influx of visitors. The inhabitants professed themselves disgusted by this invasion, but Miss Russell found it diverting. It amused her to watch the same actions performed by different people, each time as if they were doing something that had never been done before. She learnt in a few years a surprising amount about human nature.

She was not dissatisfied with her role of spectator standing on the outside of life. Her life was monotonous but quite bearable, and there were one or two little comforts she allowed herself which increased its value for her. Her cat was one. Pussy was the only creature she had permitted herself to love since her mother's death. Ostensibly acquired to keep down the mice, he became her darling, fish-fed and pampered. All the affection of her thwarted nature she could freely spill out on Pussy without fear of rebuff.

When she was in her early forties the house next door was taken by a rather showy couple called Weston. She was a lively, brassy-haired little woman with a horrid barking Pekingese that set all the neighbours complaining. And Sid Weston, her husband, who seemed quite a bit older than she was, but was just as good-natured and always ready to offer you a drink — and not lemonade, either. They were not much liked. Too rowdy, for one thing.

Living as she was next door, Kitty Weston was always bobbing in and out to borrow something from Miss Russell.

The fact was, Kitty was sorry for her.

'What a life for the old girl. It's no wonder she's grey. I'd be barmy by now if it was me. D'you know, Daddy, she's ten years older than me. You wouldn't believe it, would you?'

'You might be her daughter,' said Sid obligingly.

'It's a damn shame! I bet she's sitting there just waiting for that old man to die.'

'And then what'll she do?'

'Go wild. You'll see!'

'What's she going to use for money?'

'Oh, money!' Kitty shrugged. 'What's money . . . a herb that grows?'

'More likely end up as someone's companion.'

'Oh, shut up, Sid, you're giving me the pip. How about another teeny-weeny one before bed? Well, I'm all for a short life and a merry one. So here's to us!'

2

Death of a Cat

When Miss Russell entered the fifties she began to grudge her father every hour of life, as if it was stolen in blood and breath from her own. The cracked vase was holding together too long.

Here he was over eighty and it seemed as if he would never die. The doctor said what he had been saying for years, that he might go any time and probably would not survive his next attack, but on the other hand, with careful nursing such as he was having he might last years yet. The implication always being, of course, that Miss Russell, the ever-dutiful daughter, wished him to last as long as possible.

She scarcely acknowledged to herself her death-wish. It was really brought out into the light of day with the arrival of Nurse Dingle. The old Colonel somehow contrived to catch a cold which settled on his chest.

Tricky, at his age, and the doctor was anxious; kept him in bed and ordered a nurse. She was dreadful. Miss Russell took an instant dislike to her, seeing how the nurse openly looked down on her as a futile old maid. She had that awful brassy assurance against which snubs and the arrows of rudeness were hurled in vain. There was no chink in her starched armour. Nothing wiped off the fixed and joyless smile, or caused the determined metallic voice to waver. And her demands were endless, for this or that attention, for hot water, for some special medicament.

Miss Russell imagined that her father, who detested overbearing females, would be as irritated by her as she was. And she looked forward to a good combined grouse with him on Nurse Dingle's first day out. At least it would relieve her over-charged feelings to get something of what she felt off her chest.

Her father looked very clean and frail propped up against the white pillow.

'Well,' said Miss Russell grimly, 'how

do you like your new nurse?'

'What a charming young woman she is, always so bright and cheery, nothing's ever too much trouble.'

Miss Russell was too horrified to answer. The old man must be going senile if he can call that cow a charming young woman, she decided. Well, wild horses wouldn't drag her opinion of Nurse Dingle from her. She would talk about something else. Easier proposed than done. The old Colonel wished to talk about her, couldn't be kept off the subject at any price.

'You should have seen her face when I told her I was nearly eighty-three,' the old man chuckled. 'She said she was a pretty good judge of ages as a rule — a nurse has all kinds of ways of telling, she says, the skin, the eyes, all sorts of things — but she said she wouldn't have put me at a day over sixty-seven. What do you think of that?'

Miss Russell, longing to tell him what she thought of it, chafed inwardly. But still she was not quick enough or suspicious enough to see where this was

170

leading. She merely thought Nurse Dingle flattered him to please and soothe him, but with no ulterior motive beyond, perhaps, a nice present when she left . . . which would not be a day too soon for Miss Russell.

But it was as if there was a conspiracy about it, she hung on and hung on, and neither her father nor the doctor seemed in any hurry for her to leave.

One day she was sitting in her father's room, keeping watch over him while he slept. Nurse Dingle had taken her two hours off and on this occasion had gone into Bournemouth shopping.

Miss Russell sat there quietly with Pussy on her lap, her hand moving in steady rhythm from his ears to his tail. Presently she looked up and saw that her father's eyes were open and that he was regarding her meditatively.

'Anything you want, Father?'

He continued to gaze at her in silence, and she thought he had not heard or was not fully awake.

At last he said: 'The vicar. I want to see the vicar.'

'Whatever for?' She sprang up, letting the cat tumble with clinging claws from her lap. 'Father, you don't think . . . You feel all right, don't you?' she said anxiously.

The old man looked marvellously sly.

'It's a secret. You must promise not to tell, girl.' He tittered. 'She's shy. Promise!'

Miss Russell promised with unforced solemnity.

'Miss Dingle has done me the honour, the great, great honour to say she will be my wife.'

Miss Russell wanted to scream with laughter, to shriek, to howl, to make violent movements, to release the emotions which suddenly and painfully conflicted within her. It was too fantastic! He ought to be certified, he was dotty with extreme age. Married, at his time of life and in his state of health. The pair of them should be put away. No, she was sane enough. Crafty bitch! For there could be only one reason for her to be marrying a senile old fellow like the Colonel and that was because she knew damned well that he couldn't last above a few months, perhaps a year, and then she would be a widow with a nice little unearned income from her late husband's life insurance.

Miss Russell writhed.

'She didn't want me to tell you,' mumbled the Colonel. 'She said you'd be angry, jealous. But I said you'd have to know sooner or later if the banns go up. I want to have a special license, then we needn't be married in church. Might just as well be performed here while I'm in bed. More convenient.' He sniggered unexpectedly, and Miss Russell turned her face away, sickened. He coughed and looked solemn. 'Don't you let on you know anything to Nellie. It might upset her. She's very refined. A sensitive girl.'

'Like Mother,' suggested Miss Russell grimly, between thinned lips.

'Your mother?' The old man gazed back curiously across the years to his far away romance. 'No. Bella was a fool, she never left a chap alone, she didn't understand men. Best looking gal in India though, I was very proud of her,' he remembered.

Miss Russell, revolted, left the room.

It was lucky for her that her life's main lesson had been self-control. She was not impulsive or quick-thinking. Her thoughts moved slowly round a new idea, attacking it from every angle before she could come to any conclusion. Now, as she moved about getting the tea, she thought to herself that Nurse Dingle would be back shortly and that she must be careful to preserve an impassive face towards her.

Nurse Dingle must not be allowed to guess that the secret had been disclosed, otherwise she would be prepared and would know how to defend herself. Miss Russell must carry on just as usual.

Nurse Dingle returned with packages dangling from her little finger.

'Has he been a good boy while I've been out?'

'His tray's all ready. Perhaps you wouldn't mind pouring the water into the teapot. I'm having tea in my room. I have a headache.'

And to her surprise she found it was not a lie, she had got a headache, after all. It must be the shock, she thought, leaning back in the hard lounge-chair, a cup of strong tea on its wooden arm with three aspirins in the spoon in the saucer, and Pussy on her lap with paws drooping nonchalantly into space. What made her heart sink with fear, a fear she had never known before, was the realization that if he married, his life insurance would go to his widow, should he die without making a will, and she would be left penniless. Penniless! It struck a chill to her blood that made her shiver involuntarily. Penniless and homeless at the age of fifty-two, without talent or acquired knowledge. What would become of her? There would be no one to care what happened. She was friendless, loveless. This sudden discovery appalled her. She hugged Pussy closer for comfort and hot difficult tears of terror and self-pity dripped slowly down her cheeks. Pussy purred responsively, lashing his tail and wriggling to escape her tight pressure. His very 'livingness,' the delicious tactile sensations of smoothness, softness and warmth that he imparted, his dependence and trust in his goddess, helped to soothe and strengthen her.

If there was a way out — and they said there was a way out of every situation — she would find it. While there's life there's hope, they said. She shuddered. Funny! Funny to think that if he had died, say, this afternoon while the nurse was out . . .

Why hadn't she thought of that at the time? It would have been so easy. All she had to do when he told her the news was to make a scene, force him into a quarrel, excite him, it would not be difficult to overstrain his leaky old heart; he would have had an attack and for once the amyl-nitrate and the drops would not have been to hand. You could hardly call it murder.

The word so astonished her, jumping into her mind like that, that it quite took her breath away for a minute. Then she began busily defending herself against her own unconscious accusation. Till gradually she came round to acknowledge her long-hidden wish to kill the old man. If the Colonel should die in one of his attacks that would not surprise anybody. Yet the moment for that was past. It should have happened while Nurse

Dingle was safely out of the way. Such an opportunity might not so easily recur. Oh, what *was* she to do?

Nails tapped a light tattoo on the door. It opened a third, and Nurse Dingle slid her sheathed head through the gap.

'Dreaming in the gloaming? Head better?' She snapped on the light.

Miss Russell blinked at her. She shook herself. She had been dreaming of course and now she was awake. The dream was dispelled.

'I'm coming down to get the supper now,' she said.

But the dream was not dispelled. Though she forbade it to rise to the surface of her mind — while there were people near her, at any rate. It was as though she feared they might read her thoughts. It haunted her nightmares weirdly that night. And the next day as she worked she whistled persistently, as Tibetan monks whirl a prayer-wheel to keep evil spirits at bay.

It was a grey day, a blowy day, and in the afternoon Miss Russell decided to 'walk it off,' leaving the bloody love-birds together. Away she stumped across the flat countryside with its wide uninterrupted horizons melting from grey to grey, the trees leaning against the wind with all their leaves blown over their heads. It gave her a sense of freedom, intimations of power and energy. It made her less timorous. Instead of blowing away the dangerous thoughts, it clarified them and blew away the surrounding terrors. Death, she saw, was a trifle; it was not death that mattered but life, life that lasted but an instant against the long reign of death; but life was the conqueror, and power was the living.

The doctor would never be surprised to find him dead; he expected death to intervene at any minute, and had expected it for years (the fool!). Thank God he was a fool, Miss Russell reproved herself. It wasn't likely, in the circumstances, unless something very untoward occurred, that he would make any demur about signing the certificate. Providing it looked as though he had died of a heart attack, there was not likely to be any query. Poison, for instance. There must be poisons, if only one knew them that gave the appearance of heart-seizure. Most poisoners used arsenic or strychnine or even prussic acid. But wasn't that rather foolish? It was hardly surprising they were so easily detected, since the symptoms were unmistakable.

There must be lesser-known substances.

The lace of her brogue came undone and she knelt, frowning, in the dusty road to fasten it. Half-hidden by the long coarse grass edging the road, a little clump of wild pansies, purple and white, caught her eye. Heartsease, she thought, sentimentally preferring the old-fashioned country name. The name started a new train of thought, and she walked on more rapidly than before. Heartsease and foxglove, deadly nightshade, aconite, cow parsley and wild bryony, the words ran through her head like a fugue, telling her that every poison had its origin, and that most of them were of vegetable origin, which was going to make things so much easier for her, so very, very much easier . . .

Foxglove, for instance. They made digitalis from foxglove, she knew. And digitalis in some form or another was often prescribed for heart sufferers. She knew that, too, because the Colonel had some; she could picture the little bottle quite plainly in the medicine chest by the Colonel's bed, with its minute quantities marked so meticulously on the white label. If the contents of the bottle were untouched, no one, however nastily-minded, could suspect anything, since digitalis was unprocurable without a doctor's prescription.

When she got home she would look it up in her herbal, a charming old gardening-medical book she had picked up for tuppence years ago in Salisbury market, that was full of recipes for simple and secret distillations to relieve madness, leprosy and toothache.

But the herbal was not encouraging. Foxglove took a long time to prepare. Some other way, then. The herbal came to her assistance. (Dear little book!) There was a root, easy to acquire, easy to administer, and instantaneous in action.

'It much refembleth the horfe-radifh,' lisped the little book warningly. 'Some perfons miftaking the root of aconite for that of the horfe-radifh and ferving it as a fauce, whole families have been poifoned and killed only by tafting of it.'

The next day was Nurse Dingle's weekly day-off once again.

During luncheon, when all the neighbours would be safely indoors and there was no likelihood of spying eyes, Miss Russell went into the garden with a spade. For aconite was long-rooted and she would need to dig deeply.

She made the Colonel a nice little milk pudding for his supper, the way he liked it, with nutmeg sprinkled on top. She tied the napkin round his neck, watching his shaking old hands fumble with the spoon. She wanted to run out of the room; but couldn't move or speak — simply stared dumbly in front of her . . . paralyzed.

With the appalling timelessness of an inevitable catastrophe, the old man propelled the food towards his mouth, opened it — a dark toothless cavern of disaster, shoved in the spoonful, masticated once or twice ... and then suddenly all the veins stood out thickly like pieces of knotted string against his puckered violet skin. He gazed at his daughter in a sort of pained astonishment, stretched out one hand in an unfinished gesture, and collapsed abruptly with his head in the dish Miss Russell came back into the consciousness of her own body to find that she was as out of breath as though she had been running uphill, and that all her muscle were agonizingly tensed. Tentatively, she laid a finger on the thin tissue that covered the bones in his wrist: there was no fluttering response. The cheap clock with its loud impatient tick informed her that only a minute and a half of normal time had passed.

He was dead! Finished! She was free. An extraordinary sensation of super-sensuous exaltation pervaded her. She felt immense and omnipotent, holding the issues of life and death in her grasp. She had killed a man, and she felt marvellous.

She pulled herself together. There was

a lot to be done. And it was not a bit of use going round the place grinning like a jackass, because people would at once suspect something funny or jump to the conclusion that she had gone mad. Her feeling of superiority did not desert her as she wiped the dead man's face and laid him back on his pillows. She placed the bottle of drops and the measure on the table by his bed, as if they had been used, and broke open a capsule of amyl-nitrate. It must look as though she had done everything she could. The dish of milk pudding she carried into the kitchen and left in the sink.

Then she pulled on a coat and ran over to the house next door.

'Mrs. Weston!' she said breathlessly. 'I'm so sorry — the fact is — I wondered whether I might use your telephone . . . the nurse is out, it's her day out . . . and — and father's just died . . . ' She stood there looking distraught, because it sounded so bald said like that and she could not squeeze tears to her eyes.

'You poor kid!' exclaimed Mrs. Weston sympathetically. 'It must have given you a turn, being alone. You look all in. Come and sit down for a minute.'

'Oh no, thanks very much. I must get back. I don't like to leave him,' she said hastily, apologetically. 'I just ran over to borrow your 'phone because I thought the doctor ought to know.'

'Sid'll see to that, don't you worry . . . Sid, run and 'phone for the doctor, there's a good boy. You have Dr. Jennings, don't you? And while we're waiting you and I'll just have a little nip of brandy. You need something to pull you together. You poor dear! You'll miss him. Dear old soul, that he was. Still, it's no use pretending it's not a blessed release, and you'll see that for yourself in a little while,' she said practically, raising her glass.

She insisted on going back to the house with her, which was brave of her for she was easily scared by anything ghoulish. The doctor arrived almost at once and bore Miss Russell away to the bedroom for the last examination and the discussion of the final pitiful details.

Mrs. Weston wandered around uneasily, uncertain whether she should stay till the nurse returned or whether her duty was already accomplished and she might go. There might be something she could do for her first, she thought, switching the light on in the kitchen and gazing around her vaguely.

A fur scarf was draped carelessly over the draining-board. Funny place to leave a fur, it would get dirty there, thought Mrs. Weston, going over to pick it up and lay it somewhere else. The paws stretched out stiffly beyond the edge of the board . . . the round familiar head flung back, the mouth drooping pathetically open . . . the bold, honey-coloured eyes narrowed to a thin blue squint . . . it was horrible — but recognizably Pussy. A little bowl of some milky stuff stood in the corner of the sink. Could Pussy have been after that and suddenly been stricken? Two deaths together. Oh, horrible, horrible! Something strange . . .

'Hell!' exclaimed Mrs. Weston to herself, mysteriously agitated. 'Kitty, my girl, you'd better go home before question-time. If it's anything nasty, the less you know about it the better. And if it's funny, it's funny, and someone else can laugh at it.'

★ ★ ★

The doctor made no trouble at all: he had been expecting this for so long that he scarcely bothered to glance at the old man.

When the doctor had gone, Miss Russell walked round the house pulling the curtains. All her conflicting sensations left her feeling dazed now and tired. At first when she saw Pussy lying so still on the board by the sink she could not take in its significance. Dully she stroked the still warm little body, limp now, its whiskers be-drabbled with milk. She took him in her arms. She would have given anything for the warmth and consolation of his love just then: she felt desperately tired and empty.

Suddenly she began to cry. Pussy was dead! She was utterly bereaved and alone. The full realization of it swept over her. She sobbed for a long time despairingly, as though her grief was more than she could bear and her heart must break beneath its torrent. At last, hiccupping weakly, she dried her eyes and blew her nose. She looked at her watch. Soon Nurse Dingle would be back. And before that happened she must get rid of all traces of Pussy's sudden death.

There was still the untidy hole in the garden whence she had dug the deadly aconite, and it was easy enough to put his small body in there and drag the earth over, pressing it down firmly.

She felt so sad afterwards, so discomforted, so weary, that she had no heart to witness Nurse Dingle's reactions to the unexpected loss of her bridegroom.

Nor did it matter how much she cried within the next few days. After all, it was expected of her and considered a very suitable show of feeling. Who was to know that her tears were not for her father but for a small striped cat, with whom she had buried her heart.

3

First the Blade

It was heavenly to have the house to herself, to do things in her own time and not always be at the beck and call of a querulous invalid. She was lonely in a way, of course. She missed Pussy terribly. And the hidden knowledge that she had killed him was a guilty cicatrix on her heart like the mark of Cain. If she was haunted, it was by that.

Yes, it was lonely for Miss Russell in that house which had seemed sometimes intolerably small for two people but was now much too large for one. She still had nearly two years of her lease to run, and she could not really afford it. She advertised it to let, furnished and unfurnished, without success. It was Kitty who gave her the idea of advertising for a genial companion to share expenses.

'Lots of people would jump at the

chance of a cheap summer holiday,' she said. 'You may not find it so easy to get anyone for the winter months, but by that time something else may have turned up.'

Miss Russell was dubious.

'Well, you're not married to them. If you don't get on with them you can always tell them to go.'

Miss Russell supposed she could. Anyway, she agreed to try.

The most favourable response she had was from a Miss Combridge, an ex-Sister of a London hospital. Miss Combridge needed sea air, quiet surroundings and home cooking, and she could manage neither hotel fees nor the tension of hotel life. She had recently undergone an operation and, although it was entirely successful, aftercare was necessary. She was a good prospect to Miss Russell because, being retired, if the place suited her and they liked one another, she might stay on beyond the suggested three months, for she had given up her flatlet and was not certain that a town life would agree with her in the future.

Miss Combridge came down for a trial

fortnight. There was an unwritten agreement between them that if it proved unsatisfactory to either, the partnership should terminate at once.

Miss Combridge was older than Miss Russell, only five or six years in actual time, but considerably more in experience. At first Miss Russell thought she was going to like her immensely. After the silence and the whining it was not unpleasant to hear her loud, commanding, cheerful voice echoing from room to room. She had an apparently endless stock of anecdotes from her hospital experience, cynical and gruesome, which tickled Miss Russell's uneducated palate. And she did not shirk her share of domestic duties.

In fact, often she would take Miss Russell's job of the moment away from her insisting that she was not doing it the right way, or the best way.

Ah, that was the snag. Within a week she had altered the routine of the house to suit herself, had taken over the housekeeping on some pretext or another, and was ordering Miss Russell around.

It made Miss Russell absolutely wild, at her age and in her own house. But the woman seemed impervious to snubs and nothing she could say or do apparently had the least effect. Miss Russell decided that money or no money, companionship or not, she really could not stomach Miss Combridge's high-handed ways. There was only one thing to be done about it. She would have to ask her to leave. After seeking in vain for two or three days for a suitable opening, she decided to write a letter. She posted it to arrive the next morning, and was out the whole day on some faked-up expedition. She imagined to herself, in the bus jolting homeward, the house deliciously empty and quiet.

Her anticipations were not justified.

Her heart sank as she walked up the path and saw the lights burning through the chinks in the curtains on the ground floor.

Miss Combridge came out of the sitting-room to greet her cheerily.

'D-didn't you get my letter?' stammered Miss Russell, taken aback.

Miss Combridge laughed.

'Rather! I like you — going off for the day without a word — I must say. Lucky I'm not the kind to take offence . . . Well, we'll talk about all that after we've eaten. I expect you're pretty peckish. I am.'

The terrible woman simply refused to go. Miss Russell quarrelled with Kitty Weston about it.

'A nice mess you've landed me in, I must say,' she grumbled. 'Here she is and how am I to get rid of her, if you please? You said, 'If you don't get on with them you can always tell them to go, you're not married to them.' But I might just as well be married to her, for I don't know how to shift her.'

'Oh, how do you generally get rid of people?' Kitty flung out impatiently.

Miss Russell s fine colour faded a little and her lips trembled She swung round on her heel abruptly and strode away without another word. By the time she had got back to the house she was laughing ironically and silently. She had taken for a personal remark a general exclamation, and in consequence had nearly given the whole show away by her sudden loss of self-control. However, since the remark had not been intentional they probably had not noticed anything odd in her behaviour, or if they had they would most likely put it down to bad temper. She would smooth it over somehow the next time she saw Kitty.

The opportunity never arose. She did not chance to see either of them within the next few days. And then they were gone. They cleared out suddenly in the middle of the night with all their things, owing for six months' rent and outstanding bills to half the tradesmen round about. It made a fine scandal.

Miss Russell was on the whole not sorry they were gone. She felt safer with them out of the way. And she had not forgotten Kitty's last words to her: 'Oh, how do you generally get rid of people!' The seed had fallen on fallow ground and lay there all ready to germinate.

And still Miss Combridge stayed. Miss Russell was almost becoming resigned to the interloper in her house. Sometimes, she decided Miss Combridge was no worse than anyone else to live with, and perhaps it was all for the best that Miss Combridge had stayed.

For Miss Russell, yes, but not for Miss Combridge, who unexpectedly developed a tiresome cold which refused to be shaken off and slid down to her chest and settled there. Miss Combridge bluffly decided to ignore it and carry on as usual, with the result that in a few days she was forced to retire defeated to her bed, with a high fever and a rusty saw in her breast that went back and forth, sawing her chest in two, as she breathed.

The doctor said 'Double pneumonia,' and looked worried. So did Miss Russell, who had had quite enough of nursing, thank you. But what could you do? You would hardly turn a sick dog into the street, it simply wasn't done. She supposed glumly that it was just one more nuisance she would have to tolerate.

Miss Combridge became worse, which is hardly to be wondered at. The doctor advised a specialist. The specialist when he came looked grave.

'I — want — to — go — to — hospital,' gasped Miss Combridge, listening to the saw inside raking her more carelessly than before. The specialist took no notice.

'How is she?' Miss Russell asked later.

He shook his head.

'As bad as can be. There's no point in deceiving you. Has she no relatives . . . ? Mmm! The fact is, I don't know what to do for the best. The doctor tells me what miracles of nursing you have performed,' he said tactfully, 'but — but — might she not benefit more from the specially trained treatment she would receive in hospital?'

'I've done my best,' said Miss Russell harshly. 'She's nothing to — '

'Quite, quite,' the specialist assured her. 'My problem is whether the risk of moving her at this critical stage of the illness is justified. She does stand a better chance of recovery in hospital, I think, if the initial setback does not prove too much for her. Unless,' he mused, 'she would consider having a day and a night nurse here.'

Miss Russell was adamant on that point.

The specialist concealed his sentiments

remarkably well. In that case, the best thing he could do was to consult the sick woman herself.

Miss Combridge had no hesitation, knowing wherein she trusted. 'Hospital — hospital,' she reiterated anxiously, focusing as best she could with her glazed eyes.

'Hospital it is to be,' the specialist told Miss Russell. 'A chance in a million, I suppose.'

Miss Russell could scarcely believe that she was really going at last. And never to return. The specialist had said so. 'A chance in a million' he had said. That meant he thought she was going to die. But there was still Miss Russell's account to be settled up, and she owed her quite a bit.

She mustn't frighten her, of course, mustn't let her guess she was not coming back, Miss Russell reminded herself. But if she could just be persuaded to write a cheque for, say — no, she only needed to sign the cheque, Miss Russell could do the actual writing out. Miss Russell's honest blue eyes shone at the thought and her cheeks flushed becomingly with the increased rapidity of her heartbeats. But Miss Combridge must not be alarmed . . .

There was the specialist's fee of three guineas, Miss Russell explained. She had laid it out of course from her own purse, but if Miss Combridge felt up to signing a little cheque —

Miss Combridge stared at the wavering slip of pink paper. Pay to the order of — Miss Russell. The words slid away if she looked at them directly and she could only catch them by pretending not to look. The sum of three — what was that word?

Miss Russell's thumb was in the way — oh, guineas . . .

'Come along, dear,' urged Miss Russell, whose arm ached from propping up her almost dead-weight.

Miss Combridge regarded curiously the pen she found between her fingers and brought it to the edge of the paper with an effort.

'Too heavy,' she complained, and her head dropped to one side wearily.

Miss Russell blasphemed fervently

beneath her breath.

'I'll help you, dear,' she said. 'I'll hold your hand.' And somehow she contrived to get the signature, and a signature that despite the fever looked quite adequate. It was the refinement of cruelty, but Miss Russell would never have done it if she had not regarded it as of such importance, more important even than a dying woman's comfort. But she was not really ruthless, for as soon as it was accomplished she was all compassion and moistened the poor woman's lips with brandy, and other little ministrations. Moreover, she was so faithful to her duty that she did not even bother to look at the cheque again until the ambulance had been, and had carried Miss Combridge from her sight. Only then did she fill in the gap where her thumb had rested, with the word 'Hundred' and drew two noughts next to the figure three.

It looked all right to her. And if they did not accept it, well — She shrugged her shoulders . . . She passed it through her own bank the next day. She could never have done what she did if she had not known Miss Combridge was bound to die.

Of course Miss Combridge was bound to die — so are we all — but not just then. She recovered. Miss Russell had perhaps forgotten or underestimated her excessive will-power.

In the ordinary way, Miss Russell would have been only too pleased never to think of her again. But in these particular circumstances a little grain of uncertainty made her go to the hospital in Bournemouth on visiting days to see how she was progressing. It was soon horribly plain to her that Miss Combridge *was* progressing, instead of lapsing as the specialist had promised.

When it became clear to Miss Russell, she spent many a sleepless night wondering what she had best do. She could, she supposed dully, pay the money back into Miss Combridge's account, but that would not prevent her from knowing, or at least guessing what had occurred. It would not do. Besides, she thought indignantly, why should she give up the money? Possession, as everyone very well

199

knew was nine points of the law. There must be some other way out. There must be. And if there was it required only patience for her to find it.

It was only to be expected that Miss Combridge should return to the house for her convalescence, they were both agreed on that, and Miss Russell generously hired a car to fetch her back.

She was glad to be back, she said. She was still very weak, naturally, and she had to be put straight to bed.

The doctor came the next day and congratulated her on her miraculous recovery.

'I never thought she'd pull through,' he told Miss Russell. 'The operation she had earlier in the year told against her. Well, well, she's a plucky woman. She ought to be all right now.'

'But we can't take it for granted, I suppose. Something might still go wrong if we weren't very careful?'

'Oh lord, yes,' the doctor agreed. 'I didn't mean we could afford to take any risks. She'll need to go carefully for a good while yet.'

'Well, I'm used to taking care of people,' said Miss Russell cheerfully. 'My father was an invalid for practically thirty years and he lived to be eighty-three, with me to look after him.'

All the same, she was not going to take any unnecessary risks. She would not repeat herself and use the same methods she had used for her father. That was where cri — where people made mistakes, in repeating themselves. This time, if the worst came to the worst, the most they could say would be 'death by misadventure.'

There was a case she remembered reading in the newspaper as long ago as 1924. It had stuck in her memory because it seemed the sort of accident that could happen to anyone who did not chance to be aware of that particular danger. A woman had served stewed rhubarb leaves as a vegetable, and she and her husband and three children had all died before the doctor arrived. A tragic mistake! — that was what the coroner had said, she remembered.

A dish of rhubarb leaves boiled and

chopped up fine would look very like spinach. And what could be better than spinach for an invalid?

'Eat up your spinach, dear,' she would tell Miss Combridge.

Oh lord, how easy it was! What fools people were! Murder was as easy as snapping out a light. What a fuss people made over it. If only they knew, if only they weren't such cowards, there would be many, many more murders, she was convinced. And the exquisite and incomparable feeling of success and power it gave one! The extraordinary intensity of life one experienced; one was conscious of one's own identity as never before, a sense of intoxicating superiority. The first time it took a bit of guts to screw oneself up to the point. But after . . .

But after, Miss Russell?

Miss Combridge is dead and buried. And you have left Christbourne in search of fresh pastures and fresh victims. You know exactly what kind of victim to pick now, from all those long silent years of observation — watching the lonely little women of uncertain age with no comfort in life but their poor, meagre little savings. They are none of them missed, for they are friendless (and it was so nice for them to find a real friend at last) and who is there to notice they are gone?

But after, Miss Russell? What then?

PART THREE

WALK A LITTLE FASTER

1

Invitation to the Dance

Florence was right, Phoebe's play was a flop, after all. It limped along unnoticed for a few weeks and then quietly folded up. Phoebe was disappointed but not surprised. That was how it was in the theatre; it was impossible to gain an accurate perspective, it was all excitement and high hopes one minute and the abomination of desolation the next.

It meant that she had time now to remember Florence. She was startled and a little guilty to think how she had neglected her lately. True, she had rung up last month and left a message for Florence to 'phone her, which she had not done, but that was some time ago. Presumably she was sulking still, but it was no use to hold that against her when she was so obviously unbalanced, ill, neurasthenic.

But when Phoebe again dialled the number, the caretaker, Mrs. Bowles, told her that Florence was away, indeed had been gone some three weeks. Yes, she had her address — yes, she had heard from her, just a short letter asking for her Savings Book. But that was a couple of weeks ago now.

She gave the address to Phoebe, who wrote to her, a nice sisterly letter telling her all the gossip and hoping that she was feeling better for her holiday. Let bygones be bygones.

But day after day came and brought no letter from Florence with it. The hell with her! If she wants to sulk, let her get on with it. I've done my bit and I've nothing to reproach myself with. She dismissed the matter from her mind, as she had learnt to dismiss all tiresome and unprofitable thoughts.

All the same, during the next week it did flash involuntarily through her mind now and again to wonder what Florence was doing. She must have been really wild to have let the quarrel — the very one-sided quarrel — drag on so long.

Still, Phoebe could not see that she was to blame for it. She was willing to do anything in reason, she argued with herself, but she had her own life to consider, and was she her sister's keeper?

And then Mrs. Bowles rang her up.

'Look here, Miss,' she said, 'I don't know what to do, I'm sure. But I couldn't very well say I knew where she was, when I didn't rightly, could I? And there's her rent overdue, which I must say is most unlike her, always most punctual, she is, over that sort of thing; and the agents wanting to know every five minutes when she's going to pay, and I don't know what to tell them, except that I've had no instructions.' Here Phoebe cut in impatiently.

'I don't understand, Mrs. Bowles. What is the trouble?'

' 'Ave you heard from her, Miss? Cos I haven't had a word, not a line has she wrote me since that letter I told you of.'

'Do you mean Miss Brown?' asked Phoebe, though who else it could be she didn't know; it was some inner uneasiness that made her play for time. 'Why, no, I haven't heard from her. Perhaps she's enjoying herself too much to be bothered with writing. I'm sure she'll send the rent money though; she is, as you say, most punctilious over those things. Do tell the agents not to worry themselves, Mrs. Bowles.'

'Oh, let 'em worry, I say, the ten per cent they get off her little bit isn't going to make or break them. As for enjoying herself, well I don't know what to say about that, it wouldn't hardly do to tell that to the Firm, would it? It's the Firm I'm worrying about really — that's what made me take the liberty of ringing you up. I don't like to take the responsibility, do you see?'

'The firm?' said Phoebe. 'Do you mean where Miss Brown works?'

'That's right. They rung up this morning, Miss.'

'What did they want?'

'Goodness, Miss, I keep telling you! They wanted to know why she hadn't returned last Monday, as expected.'

'What's that?' Phoebe shouted.

Mrs. Bowles prayed for patience; really,

ladies could be very wearing, and there were her landings and the top bathroom still to be done and here she was being kept hanging on the 'phone, all out of the goodness of her heart, as it were, for anybody else wouldn't have bothered to ring up but would have let that little shrimp find her way out of her own troubles, going off like that and causing all this bother. However, she kept all those confused opinions inside her, and merely said:

'Yes, Miss, it's as I say. The Firm rang up this morning and asked to speak to Miss Brown, and I said she wasn't there. Then they wanted to know where she was, and I of course, not knowing, said she was away on holiday. They turned quite nasty then and said, Oh *was* she! And they wanted to know when she was expected back. I said I was sorry I couldn't say. All this while not understanding who they were, you see. They asked if there was anyone who did know anything, who they could speak to. Well, I wasn't going to give them your 'phone number, Miss, not likely. I thought it best to get on to you private myself, in case. And you could get on to them later if you felt so inclined.

'So I asked who was speaking and if there was any message. Then he said he was speaking on behalf of Miss Brown's Chief, who would be obliged if Miss Brown would let him know if and when she intended to return to her duties. Well, whatever could I say? I didn't want to put my foot in it, so I just said that I would give the message to Miss Brown as soon as possible and she would get in touch with them. And that was that. Except that I thought you ought to know, and anyway you might have heard from her, but even if you hadn't you'd know what to do better than I should.'

'Oh yes, Mr. Bowles, very sensible of you — '

'And I didn't forget to tell him that she was taking the holiday by doctor's orders, either. Well, I wasn't going to let him come the acid over me. No fear!'

'You say, they said she was expected back last Monday. And today is Friday. That seems very odd, doesn't it?' Phoebe was too perturbed to give Mrs. Bowles the full dose of admiration she required. She wanted to comprehend where the mistake lay.

'Odd, Miss? Well, I don't know why she never came back, I'm sure, and you may call that odd if you like. For she was expected back last Monday — well, back at the business on Monday, but I expected her back the Saturday previous as it happened. Four weeks, I understood, she was to be away. And I did think it funny when she never turned up and when I never heard nothing, either — '

'Why ever didn't you tell me before, then?' wailed Phoebe.

'I wasn't to know that you hadn't heard, was I, Miss,' Mrs. Bowles said reasonably. 'It was hardly my place . . . And then the agents fussing about the rent and saying they'd have to let the room to someone else, and then these people 'phoning today, made me feel that it really was up to her family to deal with it.' Her tone was the least bit querulous. 'So I rang you up.'

'Yes, quite right, quite right, Mrs.

Bowles. I only meant that I wish I had known before, in case she's been taken ill again, you know. However, it's done now, so never mind. Could I have that address again, please?' She noted it down on the pad beside the telephone, thanked Mrs. Bowles effusively once more, and rang off.

Today was as good a day as any to go down to Brighton and pay Florence a surprise visit. She hoped Florence wasn't ill again. She hoped Florence would be pleased to see her. Again she felt faintly uneasy, wondering what Florence had been doing with herself for a month.

Phoebe found the Belleview Hotel after some difficulty, up a side turning on the way to Kemp Town. It had an unspeakably depressing air and smelt stuffy. The lounge-hall was dark with plush and empty. The thought of her own sister, of any human being, having to live in such a place struck dismay to Phoebe's heart. It would be impossible for anyone to live there, it would be a mere creeping existence, a dead horror.

She paced up and down disgustedly,

hardly venturing to breathe the fetid air. Where was everyone? Was there no one to attend to business? Were they all dead? She struck the bell on the narrow reception desk three times, impatiently. It was hateful to think of Florence staying in such a place for a day, much less a month. She was painfully aware that if she had gone with her, she would have seen to it that they stayed somewhere bright and comfortable.

She resumed her angry striding. Her irritable thoughts brought her to a standstill before the green baize letter-rack on the wall. Her eyes traced unseeingly the crisscrossed braiding and the diamond-angled envelopes beneath them. Suddenly the words *Miss Florence Brown* jumped out at her from an oblong white envelope.

She bent forward. Why, it was her own handwriting! It was her own letter to Florence! But why —

A voice behind her said:

'Can I assist you, madam?'

She whirled round to face a poker of a woman with a frightened, venomous

expression behind her steel-rimmed spectacles.

Phoebe said, with a nervous laugh:

'Oh, yes, I want to see my sister, Miss
Brown.'

The woman was silent for a full minute
before she said that she was sorry but
there was no one there of that name. She
eyed her spitefully, pinching in her lips.
She knew what that type was after, thanks
very much; common as brass, with all
that dyed hair, and smiling all over her
face.

'Oh, but you must be mistaken. I know
she is here.'

'No one of that name,' the woman
insisted, pleased to be mean to the warm
and charming creature before her. It was
hard to believe, looking at them, that they
must be about the same age. 'Perhaps you
have the wrong address,' she suggested, as
Phoebe did not move.

'Why, no. Besides — ' she indicated the
letter-rack, tapping her letter with an
enamelled nail 'that *is* my sister,' she
smiled gently.

The woman looked taken aback; thrust

her nose right up against it in order to scrutinize suspiciously the postmark.

'But this is a fortnight old.'

'I know. I wrote it myself.'

'Oh well,' said the woman patronizingly, 'that would account for it. It's as I say, you see, you have the wrong address.'

'I'm sure I'm not mistaken,' said Phoebe in bewilderment.

'Well, we haven't anyone of that name staying here.'

'Perhaps you wouldn't mind looking to make sure.'

What impudence, thought the woman. 'I suppose I am allowed to know what visitors we have.'

'Nevertheless,' said Phoebe, suddenly regal, 'I should be obliged if you would look in your register.'

And there was nothing for it but to turn over the ledger and prove to the creature that there were no Browns staying there. But there it was, funnily enough, after all, Miss F. Brown, Arkwright Road, London. Well, if that wasn't queer! And she would have sworn —

But the lady was asking questions (she

had jumped in an instant, because she had been right all the time, from a 'creature' to a lady) and subdued now, ashamed of her previous rudeness, she fetched the proprietress.

Mrs. Cusack presented herself blandly. A mountainous woman with a large puffy face and eyes that glinted sharply behind her pince-nez, she suggested a horribly humanized mouse.

Why, no, she was sorry she did not know where Miss Brown had gone. She had left no address. She had only stayed a few days. And really they had so many visitors, coming and going all the time . . . Mrs. Cusack contrived to give the impression that the place was in a constant whirl of arrivals and departures; but the truth was that she did not even remember Miss Brown. She hardly ever directly observed the guests; and Florence was not very likely to attract notice. So she was not able to tell Phoebe much, and in the end she had to go away bewildered and unsatisfied. Where was Florence? It was very remiss of her to run away like this without a word; thoughtless and unkind, leaving people to worry.

When she got back to London she went straight up to Arkwright Road before going home. She was reasonably self-contained as a rule, but she must have felt more uneasy than she acknowledged, for she was nervously impelled to discuss it with someone: and in the circumstances who could be better for that purpose than Mrs. Bowles.

'But it does seem funny, doesn't it?' she said plaintively, sipping dark bitter tea in Mrs. Bowles' basement parlour, for Mrs. Bowles seemed curiously disinclined to give an opinion. She had exclaimed suitably at first, and shown the letter where she asked for her Savings Account book, and then she folded her hands in her lap and nodded her head solemnly from time to time, but would not venture an opinion.

So for the third time Phoebe suggested that it was funny.

At which Mrs. Bowles heaved up a sigh from the depths of her stomach and said, Yes and No, and perhaps it would be best if she told all and then Mrs. Moore could judge for herself. Whereupon, she told Phoebe of Florence's attempted suicide and of how she had saved her and called in the doctor and how the doctor had taken her away to a place in the country. And this time was Phoebe's turn to listen in silence. When Mrs. Bowles ceased talking, there was quite a silence between them.

Phoebe was profoundly shocked. She felt sick and hurt at her own inadequacy; to think that Florence had walked out of her flat and gone straight home to kill herself. And all this while she had known nothing of it. Her own sister! It was horrible!

'Why didn't you tell me?' she groaned.

'Well, Miss, I couldn't tell you when you rang up because I didn't know, then, myself. And after, there was too much to see to. And next day Miss Brown didn't say nothing, and wouldn't ring you up, and it seemed hardly my place. I thought the doctor would say whatever was necessary. It was an awkward situation for all concerned, Miss; and I had to remember that if it got known I might find myself looking for another job . . . Oh, and talking of that, Miss, reminds me that a parcel came for her a while back, and I believe it was addressed in her own handwriting. It's in her room: should I run up and fetch it?'

'I'll come with you, Mrs. Bowles. I want to have a look round her room.'

It was neat enough but for a film of dust, for which Mrs. Bowles apologised, although cleaning her ladies' rooms was no part of her business unless she was paid extra for it. Phoebe opened drawers and doors. Florence had not taken many clothes with her, she noticed, but then she had not many clothes altogether.

She scrutinized the parcel. It was just possible to decipher the blurred post mark as Patchet, Sussex.

'Patchet?' mused Phoebe, frowning. 'Never heard of it . . . I think I'll open this, Mrs. Bowles — there may be something inside which will give us a hint.'

But, on the contrary, it only served to deepen the mystery. For all it contained was a dark blue towel. And what could be the significance of that, pray? Queer!

'Well!' exclaimed Mrs. Bowles. 'Whatever next! That is a surprise and no mistake!'

'And the moral of that is — ?' said Phoebe, who when perplexed often quoted 'Alice in Wonderland' to herself. For why all the mystery?

If Florence was merely indulging in a harmless holiday, why not say so? Why not write to someone and tell them about it? Why the secrecy? Why in heaven's name had she not returned when she was expected? And why no word to her employers, her only living relative, or her landlady?

'Thank you so much for all the trouble you've taken,' she said, as she pressed Mrs. Bowles' hand; but her face was pale and troubled.

The next person to be seen was Dr. Paget. They were not strangers, but Phoebe did not care for him over-much, thinking him an old fogey and feeling that he must disapprove of her.

She apologised prettily for taking up his time in consulting hours and explained that she had come about her sister.

'Ah yes,' he said genially. 'And how is she getting on?'

'I'm afraid I don't know.' She looked at him fixedly. 'I haven't seen or heard from her since the day before she tried to kill herself.'

'Dear me,' he said. 'Yes, that was a bad business. And you haven't heard from her? How is that?'

'I don't know. We had a bit of a row that day. She wanted me to go away with her and I couldn't, it wasn't convenient just then; and she became bitterly angry with me and walked out. That was the last I heard of her. No one has told me anything. I've been kept completely in the dark all this while. It wasn't till today that I learnt she had tried to kill herself. And then this caretaker person, where she lives, told me you took her away into the country somewhere. But why I've not been told anything of all this is more than I can understand.'

Her tone was accusing.

He muttered something about a patient's sacred confidences. One had to consider one's patient's well-being first and foremost, and he felt it to be to Miss Brown's advantage to accede to her wish that nothing of what had happened should be mentioned to *anyone*. He underlined the last word with his voice. He did the best for her he knew by taking her down to this very pleasant convalescent home in Brighton.

'Well, she evidently didn't like it there, for she went to stay at a boarding house. A horrible place,' added Phoebe. 'If your convalescent home was no better than that, I'm not surprised she left it. And now she's left that place too, and we don't know where she is. It is not only that she's written to no one, but what makes me so worried is that she should be back at work by now and they have been inquiring about her. I don't know what to say to them. It isn't likely that they will hold her job open indefinitely, even with her record of service, because she has been giving them a lot of trouble lately, one way and another. And if she loses this job, goodness knows if she'll ever get another. What am I to do for the best?'

He agreed the situation was bad, difficult. He questioned her adroitly, until he knew as much of the affair as she did.

'If only I had known about this suicide business,' lamented Phoebe, 'I would never have let her go away alone. Oh, she was always talking about it, I know; but I never thought for a moment that she'd go so far as to try it. I didn't think she'd have the guts, for one thing. And then they say that people who talk about it never mean to do it.'

'So you think she has gone off somewhere to kill herself in hiding?' suggested Dr. Paget.

She glanced at him sideways, with a scared look.

'That is what I'm afraid of,' she whispered.

He smiled confidently.

'I think not. I'll get in touch with the Matron of the convalescent home and find out what happened, and then I'll let you know.'

Phoebe, disliking his assurance, said sharply she would prefer to deal with it herself. If Dr. Paget would be so good as to let her have the address, she would contact them as soon as possible.

'Just as you like, of course. I am confident that Miss Brown has not taken her own life,' he euphemized. 'Remember the Savings Book, Mrs. Moore, remember the Savings Book.'

Old fool, Phoebe thought, as she walked away. Who does he think he is — Sherlock Holmes? Before she did anything else though, she must ring up Browne, Hoggers & Whiteley and ask to speak to Mr. Hoggers, Florence's Chief. She concocted some fairly plausible excuse that ought to hold them for a few days more, at least, and by that time she considered she would have found out her sister's whereabouts.

Only then did she turn her footsteps in the direction of the local police station, situated in a drab little street at right angles to the back of the block of flats where she lived.

She glanced round the dingy room. It was empty but for a very young policeman, writing laboriously, as though he was still in the schoolroom.

'I want to see the Chief Constable,' she remarked imperiously.

The very young policeman smiled in spite of himself. Fancy asking to see a Chief Constable in a local metropolitan station! He tried to explain to the lady that Superintendent Brady was at the head of their station.

'Very well. I'll see the Superintendent.'

He bit his lip in the effort not to laugh again,

'The Superintendent's out. I'm sorry,' he blurted.

'I hope you're not trying to be funny,' she said severely. 'There must be someone in this station with better manners than you, and whoever they are I wish to see them.'

The very young policeman blushed, and shuffled his feet.

'Yes, ma'am,' he agreed. 'I'll tell Inspector Johnson,' and he dived through an adjacent doorway to merciful oblivion.

Inspector Johnson proved to be a hearty gentleman with a twinkling eye and a velvety voice. He pushed forward a chair welcomingly, and then leant back in his own and placed the tips of his fingers together, lawyer-fashion, surveying her speculatively through half-closed eyes. And charming she looked, sitting there so gracefully on the upright chair, her hands joined loosely in her lap, her face solemn and childlike between the softly falling red locks.

She began thoughtfully: 'I've lost my sister . . .'

He listened patiently, asking questions from time to time and making notes on a pad for the official description . . . Height: four foot ten. Complexion, sallow. Hair, black; and eyes grey. No distinguishing marks. Last seen wearing — ?

But Mrs. Moore did not know, had not thought to ask Mrs. Bowles; but she guessed she was probably wearing navy, a dress and a long coat, and — well — a black hat and black court shoes.

'And so far as you know she was last heard of in the Brighton district sometime last month, you don't quite know when, but about three weeks ago, you think. Is that right?' The Inspector spoke as he wrote. He blotted the sheet and looked up. 'We shall first get in touch with the hospitals — ' She blenched, and he added calmly: 'It quite often happens that people are knocked down and subsequently lose their memories. We try that first because it is common,' he explained. 'But there may well be some less drastic explanation of your sister's disappearance. 'We shall send this description to all local and district police stations. And if she's drawn money from the post office on her Savings Account . . . Well, I will let you have a report in a few days, Mrs. Moore.' He rose, and she held out her hand.

'It isn't like her, you know, to disappear into the blue this way,' she couldn't refrain from saying.

'I wonder if you have any idea how many people disappear in England in a year. But they turn up again in a few weeks — generally in a few days when the case has been given to the police. We're fairly spry, you know. I really don't think you need worry, Mrs. Moore.'

But Phoebe, who had kept back the attempted suicide, lest the police might punish Florence for it later, could not help worrying. And then the report when it came was not so very satisfactory.

They had obtained from G.P.O. the serial number of Miss Brown's Savings Account book and by means of that had traced it to the post office at Liverpool, where the entire contents had been withdrawn and the account closed.

'But — what does it mean?' A frown puckered Phoebe's white brow. 'I don't understand. Why should she do that?'

'Liverpool,' said Inspector Johnson. 'I don't think there can be much doubt about it. She must have wanted to make a clean break. Drew out all her money, bought a ticket and has sailed off, probably to the States.'

Phoebe stared at him, thunderstruck, her soft full lips apart.

'The last thing in the world she'd do,' she said emphatically.

'Ah, you're surprised,' he noted phlegmatically. 'But you never can tell what people are going to do. Human beings are the most unaccountable creatures, most unaccountable.'

'And none more so than my sister,' she acknowledged. 'But she wouldn't do that. She'd never have the pluck, for one thing.'

Inspector Johnson looked at her kindly.

'She may not have gone alone, you know. We have to consider that.'

It took Phoebe a minute or two to realize that he meant she had run away with a man. She burst out laughing.

'Oh, my dear man, you couldn't be further from the mark! Florence — well, if you'd seen her; but I don't mean her looks, either, it was just that she was so shut up in herself, she hated people, she was frightened of them. No, no, she would never have gone away with a man.'

Inspector Johnson was unmoved.

'You know, Mrs. Moore, you would be astonished if I told you that families nearly always say pretty much word for word what you have said, and yet nine times out of ten it proves to be the case. They say that husbands or wives are always the last persons to know of their partner's infidelities, don't they, and I think much the same thing occurs in families. A curious kind of secrecy, almost of jealousy, prevails.'

'I can only repeat that I cannot believe it.'

The Inspector sighed. 'The money was withdrawn nine days ago. It is possible, if I am right in my surmise that she has gone to America that she will write to you to let you know she has arrived safely. So you may hear soon.'

Phoebe nodded coolly.

'If I do, I shall certainly let you know,' she promised, with her sweet and dangerous brogue. Fat old fool, she thought, do you think I don't know my own sister! A lot of good you are, you police. I shall find her myself.

And why not? She had quite a lot to go on. There was the mysterious postmark of Patchet, for one thing. She'd like to know more about that. She did not even know where Patchet was, except that it lay somewhere behind the Sussex downs.

She found, also, by experience the next day, that it was nearly three miles from the railway station; but the sky was high and a fine vaporous blue, the air full of warm country scents, and she enjoyed the walk.

She wandered up the village street. There were only two pubs, one possible and the other impossible. Over a lunch of bread and cheese and ale at the possible inn, she discussed trade with the landlord. They had a 'commercial' in for a night now and again, or a honeymoon couple in the summer, it being quiet and off the beaten track, but otherwise they didn't do much in the hotel line. No, they had had no one recently.

Where else could one stay here? Phoebe asked. The landlord shook his head. There was nowhere else. Some of the cottagers took in visitors 'to oblige,' but though they were clean enough, he would hardly dare recommend them to a lady who probably liked her bath every day. Or else, he suggested, wiping down the counter mechanically, there was Lewis, the estate-agent, he might have something to offer.

She did not really see how the estate-agent could help her, but she did not relish the idea of trundling from cottage to cottage, questioning suspicious villagers on their own doorsteps, and decided to try him first . . . Mr. Lewis was thin and beery, with a ragged yellow moustache. It was a nice change for him to see a pretty lady, and he practically welcomed her with open arms.

'I'll be perfectly frank with you,' she said ingenuously. 'I have not come on business. I thought you might be able to help me find an old friend of mine. I'm certain she's living in Patchet because I heard from her the other day. But unfortunately I mislaid the letter with the address on it, and I don't know how I'm to get hold of her. I thought you would be the person to help me because you would be certain to know where everyone lives.'

Mr. Lewis rocked back and forth violently in his chair and, offering her a cigarette, lit one for himself.

'Now, this friend, this friend — I take it she hasn't been here long? Rented a house, you think? Well, that's easy then. I have only rented one house here — I mean, strictly *here*, of course — I have business all over Sussex, oh, dear me, yes

— but *here*, I have only actually rented one house, one cottage, I might more truthfully say, in the last five months. To a Mrs. Jolly. Would that be your friend?'

'A dark lady, very small,' said Phoebe, dubiously.

'Ah no, then it isn't the same person. My client was biggish and elderly, evidently someone else.'

'My friend might be staying with her. I can't be certain that she's alone . . . It is rather important,' she added plaintively.

'We could go and see,' he admitted, and plucked a lavender Trilby off the hat stand.

He tried to pump her discreetly as they walked down the High Street, but she was too wary for him. She talked of property, of how much she would like a little country cottage she could retire to when the world became too much for her.

They stood outside the funny little cottage and waited. It seemed no one was in. Peering in at the windows, the place looked quite uninhabited. The whole thing was rather footling after all; a dead end. She felt depressed. Wasn't she rather stupid to have wasted her time on a goose's errand? She moved away from the window. A clot of mud from the flowerbed she had trodden on adhered to the toe of her shoe. It stuck obstinately, despite her stamping. In it was half-buried a cigarette end that someone must have tossed out of the window at some time or another. Even from there she could see the brilliant stamped trademark on the butt that signified a de Bris cigarette. Phoebe always teased Florence for smoking them, and said debris was just about what they were made of.

There must be hundreds of thousands of other people who smoked de Bris cigarettes besides Florence, she told herself. But in spite of her cool reasoning it seemed more than a coincidence.

She returned to the flowerbed and pushed the bushy wallflowers this way and that, inquisitively. Something gleamed. She picked it up with a little crow of surprise and delight. A key! Front door? Back door? Easy enough to find out, surely.

She felt that she must see inside the cottage now. Using all her appeal, she explained to Mr. Lewis how much she desired to see the cottage, how adorable it appeared to her, and how much she would like to rent a cottage like this when his client's lease ran out. If it were possible just to peep inside —

Mr. Lewis, feeling immensely gallant and capable, decided it was possible and ushered her in. Obviously Mrs. Jolly was not there; she may have been there but she was so no longer. Everything was tidy, empty, and closed. The place smelt stuffy, and fading sunlight beamed through the dancing dust. Could Florence have been here? The place might never have been habited. A God-forsaken, uninviting hole, Phoebe considered it. Not so much as a scrap of paper to hint at anything, she thought disgustedly, mounting the rickety staircase. The bedrooms were sparsely furnished, the beds unmade. 'Annie doesn't live here anymore,' murmured Phoebe. And then she saw the mirror turned with its face to the wall. Why did that call up Florence so clearly to her? Suddenly, she was convinced that Florence *had* been here. Something of her atmosphere seemed to have remained in that bare shabby room, something doleful and afraid. She remembered Florence as she had last seen her a pathetic little object, crouching by the window and saying, 'I'm afraid, I'm afraid.' Ah, that was it! She had it now! Memory swung into place and she heard Florence telling her why she had turned Phoebe's mirror face to the wall: it *frightened* her. And here! — Oh, that could hardly be a coincidence!

Mr. Lewis was fidgeting in the doorway. She could have no excuse for lingering like this.

She wondered whether she might not find a possible explanation of the ink-stained towel here. It would be just like Flo to get in a panic over a thing like that. In the linen cupboard was a pile of red-bordered towels similar to the blue-stained one Florence had sent home. If only she had some excuse to count the linen, but the most she could do on that score was to ask Mr. Lewis to let her know later of what the household linen consisted, for she did so hate to be short, and if she took the place she would sooner bring down some of her own things with her than never have sufficient.

'Sure to be half-a-dozen of everything,' Mr. Lewis assured her.

'Sure to be,' she agreed, 'but when I peeked in the linen cupboard just now it seemed to me very short of towels.'

But if Florence had been here and it was not just a crazy dream of hers, where did this Mrs. — Mrs. Jolly come in? Who was she? What did Mr. Lewis know about her?

Really nothing beyond what he had already told her, when it came down to it. He had seen her once only and that for a very short time. And the fact was she was not the sort of person who was very distinctive — he glanced at Phoebe admiringly and pulled at the ends of his moustache — and he did not think he would know her if he saw her again.

'She was just like everybody else. Ordinary. I don't know where women get those sort of clothes that look as if they've never been new. Look as if they were born in them, those sort of women do. You go to any cathedral town you like on a market day: the streets are full of 'em, full of 'em. And you can't tell one from the other.'

There was just time to catch the hourly bus to Brighton, where she had tea and then stepped out for the convalescent home in Hove, whose address the doctor had given her.

2

Tread Softly

The matron of the Convalescent Home was a brisk competent woman. She did recall Miss Brown but you could see the recollection displeased her; the episode had been a failure and the memory rankled. Still, she did her best to be helpful.

Mrs. Moore's sister, was it? A sad case, she was sure. She had just walked out one day and sent for her luggage. Yes, there had been a letter. Now, what had she done with it?

'It was from her aunt. I remember now. Funny how things come back to you.'

'An aunt?' Phoebe frowned, and checked herself from saying, 'But we haven't got an aunt!'

The matron eventually retrieved the letter, having filed it away under some hopelessly unorthodox system, and handed it to Phoebe. It was from the Hotel Metropole and was signed by a Miss Emma Brown. But what a farrago of nonsense!

'Who came for the luggage?'

The Matron believed, yes, she was certain, that it was a messenger boy. Phoebe asked to be allowed to take the letter away with her. It did not seem quite fair, but the Matron could not think of any legitimate objection on the spur of the moment.

Phoebe came away well pleased with her piece of evidence: but evidence for what or against whom she could not have told you. Was Florence *Emma Brown*? Was that a ruse of hers for getting away? It was not impossible. But at the Hotel Metropole they had no trace of an Emma Brown or a Florence Brown, nor even, as a last hope, of a Mrs. Jolly. Nor were Phoebe's descriptions of any use.

'But this is your notepaper,' she asserted.

Oh, undeniably it was. But — here the manager shrugged plump shoulders — what was to prevent a client taking some away with him? Many of their clients did, people liked to get something for nothing; and as for the management, they did not care, for it was all good advertisement. It could even have been written by someone who was not staying in the hotel. It was impossible for the house detectives to watch *everyone*. He regretted his inability to be of more use to her.

She tried next the detestable Belleview Hotel. She asked to see the proprietress, Mrs. Cusack. And Mrs. Cusack, who liked to have a nice port-and-lemon in peace, at this time of day, came and stared at her blankly, unhelpfully.

'I came here a few days ago about my sister, Miss Brown. You may remember.'

'Last week,' concurred Mrs. Cusack, folding her thick white paws together and staring at a point beyond Phoebe's shoulder.

'I am still trying to contact her. And it occurred to me — I wondered whether you had a Mrs. Jolly calling here for her. She may even have stayed here, for all I know.'

'Never heard the name,' said Mrs. Cusack firmly.

'An elderly lady, she would be,' Phoebe tried helpfully.

Mrs. Cusack shook her head.

'A biggish person. Dressed — ordinarily.'

Mrs. Cusack shook her head.

Phoebe ran her tongue over her lips.

'Or a Miss Emma Brown?'

'Here!' cried Mrs. Cusack, 'what is this — a game? How many more people are you going to ask after, I should like to know! Have you lost *all* your relations?'

'No,' said Phoebe pleasantly. 'But they are all connected with my sister, and I believe that they were also down here at the time. It surely isn't anything so very extraordinary.'

'Well, I don't know,' Mrs. Cusack said doubtfully. 'It wouldn't be a divorce case, now, would it? We don't care for that sort of thing at all. We've a name for respectability.'

Phoebe reassured her. She was sure that Mrs. Cusack could help her if she would only bend her purpose to it. Surely there must be one member of her staff who would remember waiting on Miss

Brown, would remember some incident about her, would remember when she left. Phoebe could be very persuasive, and she had to overcome the ugly old monster's instinctive dislike and suspicion of her. Mrs. Cusack in desperation, more to be rid of her than anything else, called to a passing house-boy: 'Jim! Come here a minute.'

He came up obediently, like a cheerful wooden toy, with a head as round and shining as a ball.

'This lady would like to ask you some questions,' said Mrs. Cusack. And that really was the utmost she was prepared to do, she could not waste any more time on this tiresome creature.

'See that you answer them properly,' she said severely, and rolled out of sight behind layers of dusty velvet portieres.

And, strangely enough, Jim did remember Miss Brown leaving. He himself had put her luggage in the car.

'Car?'

'Yus. A dark green Austin.' His little black eyes twinkled. 'Number YMZ23109,' he added.

But he couldn't possibly have memorized the car number, thought Phoebe. Such things didn't happen in real life. Why should he have remembered it, anyway? Unless — unless there was something so very unusual about it (about the whole affair, she meant) that he had fixed it in his mind deliberately.

'What makes you so certain of the number?'

He polished his red cheek with the back of his hand.

'It's like this, lady,' he said, in the manner of one embarking on a saga. 'I live with my married sister and my bruvver-in-law's got a little garage, see. Well, I like to give him a hand whenever I can, an' I know pretty much what he's got down vere. Not long ago he part-exchanged an Austin for an old Ford. It was a good deal. And togever, we made a tidy little job of ve Austin. Ve number was YMZ23109 — like I told you. Course, when I saw it again I remembered it at once.'

'And who did your brother-in-law sell it to, do you know?'

But he could not help her there. Nor had he noticed the driver. Why should he? His bruvver-in-law might be able to help her. Phoebe gratefully took down the car number and the address of the garage, and pressed a suitable coin into Jim's ready palm in recognition of his useful memory.

Jim's brother-in-law, a stout, affable man, leant up against a petrol pump and exclaimed admiringly, 'That kid's as smart as you make 'em. He'll get on in the world, you see if he don't.'

As to the party he sold the Austin to — he scratched his head thoughtfully . . . as near as he could remember, it was a middle-aged party, that is to say he'd guess she was nearer sixty than fifty. Ho, yes, she was a lady, all right, and knew her own mind. No, he hadn't not to say noticed anything partickler about her; just like everybody else, she seemed to him. Well, no, he didn't think he would know her again if he saw her, not to say for certain, like. Still, that kid, Jim, was right about the car number, any old how. And he had only to turn up his ledger to see the date he sold it to her, if that was any use. Always ready to oblige . . . Sorry not to be more helpful . . . Any time she wanted to hire a car . . .

But Phoebe was not dissatisfied with her work. Police, she thought scornfully, don't talk to me about the police! I've found out more in one day than they discovered in a week. Fools, incompetent fools!

Who, she wondered on her way back to London, was this mysterious woman? Was she a friend of Florence's? Florence always made out that she had no friends. Was she someone from the office? Or someone Florence had met on this last excursion? And who was Emma Brown? Were Emma Brown and Mrs. Jolly the same person? It was odd, uncanny. Though Florence had always been secretive by nature there had never been anything unaccountable, never anything really to be hidden. Why had Florence left that nursing-home without a word, without paying her bill or anything? That was unlike her, too. Was it prearranged with this Mrs. Jolly or Madam X, or whoever she was? All this swift moving about: first the nursing-home, and then after a couple of days the Belleview Hotel, and then again a few days later she went off in a car, presumably to Patchet, where again she can only have remained a short while: and then . . . where? Phoebe shivered uneasily.

Florence hated change. Wasn't that one of her main reasons for not wishing to take this enforced holiday? What in heaven's name had prevailed on her to suffer all this moving about? There must have been some strong urge . . . Again Phoebe shivered. Where was Florence now? Could that wretched Inspector creature be right after all, could she have boarded a liner for the States or South America, perhaps in the company of Madam X? Oh, the idea was farcical! She dismissed it crossly from her thoughts.

All the same, she went round to the police station that evening after she had eaten and bathed. She had the impulse to boast a little of her work.

But she was not to enjoy her little triumph. When she arrived at the station it was to find the Inspector out on a case. It was nice to know he did some work, Phoebe thought sourly, obscurely disappointed. She had looked forward to his surprise at her ingenuity, perhaps he would have commended her, or better still he might have been angry, then she would know she had been really smart, smarter than the police. How childish she was being! Everyone knew the English police were the most thorough and the least corrupt in the world. Why could she not be patient? She had no reason to believe they had closed the case; it was quite possible that they were still investigating or waiting for further information to turn up. Well, she would provide them with some. And at the same time it would serve to show that she had been up to something and that the grass would never grow under her feet.

She smiled charmingly at the policeman on duty in the corner of the room, scribbling beneath a green-shaded lamp.

'Will you tell Inspector Johnson that — in connection with my sister's disappearance — there is a car number, YMZ23109.

It was a dark green Austin. Driven by — no, never mind that, just tell him the number, will you? You won't forget?'

Inspector Johnson found the message when he got back to the station about half-past ten that night, tired from unsuccessful work. He was not interested in the particular bit of routine work he had on hand; it may not have been surprising that his mind was not in it, but it was rather more surprising that his thoughts reverted so often to Phoebe. He had never been a womanizer, though there had once been somebody — but, ah, he would not think about her even now, and ever since then he had concentrated on his work rather than frivolity. After all, he was no longer young, and he certainly wasn't anything to look at and he wasn't clever, just a plodding ass of a police inspector, and one might as well be an inspector of drains for all the romance-appeal there was in that. Oh, he could have married easily enough, there were plenty of serious little women who would have been only too pleased to settle down. But there was an odd streak of romance in this common-sensible man and he still retained a respectful, an ardent, a youthful attitude towards 'love.' To marry without love merely for the sake of companionship seemed unnatural and pathetic to him. Marriage in itself, then, was not such a desirable state, though yes, he did sometimes feel lonely in his bachelor digs.

But Mrs. Moore? Where did she come in? Through some defenceless cranny in his brain, evidently, for at the oddest moments he would see her before him, her long cameo-white face with the pale bluish-green eyes set at a slant, and the troubling mouth like a bruised flower; her quiet dignity in such contrast with her wild red hair. It was like being haunted. The vision only lasted a second or so at a time — just long enough for him to lose the thread of what he was thinking or saying.

He never thought about her consciously. Mrs. Moore? Who was she? She had never mentioned her husband, but presumably she had one. And in that case he had no business whatsoever to be having visions — in the body or out of the body — of someone else's wife.

Perhaps that accounted for his depression that evening. Certainly he experienced a vivid lightening of heart when he found she had been in — even though he had missed her — for he had not thought to see her again, and after all she had come back and left a message for him. And what a curious message! No. YMZ23109.

Now, what had she been up to? He could make that an excuse to go round and see her when he came off duty. Except that midnight was hardly the hour to choose for one's first call on a lady, especially when one was uninvited. No, if she had wanted to see him she would have said so, or mentioned that she would call in the next day. How had she come by that car number? Why had she left only the bare bones, as it were, of this new discovery instead of letting him know how she had attained her knowledge? Perhaps she had some special reason for not wishing him to know the details. Or perhaps she was annoyed . . . perhaps it was done deliberately to spur him on. He laughed without rancour. Well, if she wanted the car traced, he would trace it for her — tomorrow. That was something to look forward to as he strode through the dark streets still glistening with recent rain. But to Miss Brown he never gave a thought.

He sent out a query to all counties the next day. And while this routine inquiry was proceeding methodically to its appointed end, Phoebe had a piece of luck, the first piece of luck — if that was the word for it — that she had had since she lost touch with her sister.

Walking down a turning off Lamb's Conduit Street her eye was attracted by a little tapestry chair in the window of a junk shop. It was one of those dirty old dens where articles are as surprisingly juxtaposed as in a surrealist picture: a battered harp, a chamber, a pair of corsets, a toasting-fork, a soiled card announcing that they would pay high prices for your gold, silver, and unwanted false teeth. The chair was half-concealed behind these objects, but Phoebe could see that the frame was unmistakably Chippendale and she hesitated, wondering whether it was worthwhile going in to inquire the price. Her glance ran appraisingly over the objects tossed higgledy-piggledy into the window, gauging their value, when her eye was caught and held by something familiar.

Suddenly she realized what it was and peered at it more intently. It was a small miniature brooch, edged with a ribbon of blue enamel starred with marquisate. A pretty little thing, and as familiar to her as her own hand. There could not be two of them. And this had surely belonged to her mother. Why, she could still see it fastened in the ruffles at her mother's neck. And when her mother died and her few possessions had been divided up, this brooch had gone to Florence. It was practically her only decent piece, and she wore it on every possible occasion.

Arriving at this point in her sequence of thought, Phoebe plunged into the murky shop with a vehemence that sent all its glass bells jangling. To the pallid little woman with a scarf tied round her head, who appeared from the dark recesses, she said:

'May I see that brooch, the miniature brooch, you have in the window?'

But when she had it in her hands she received no additional assurance from it. The picture was as she remembered it, but she was not certain any longer of the number of stars that edged it, there were only five on this and she had the impression that her mother's had more. Memory was inadequate on these details. There was no photo in the locket part at the back, as she had hoped. Could she have made a mistake? Would Florence ever have sold it?

'Have you had this long?'

The woman, patient and inattentive, said soothingly:

'Oh, yes, Madam.'

'I wonder if you can tell where you bought it,' said Phoebe in her most persuasive-manner.

'I'm afraid I couldn't. My husband sees to all that,' she excused herself glibly.

'Is your husband in? I'd like to speak to him.'

'I'm afraid he is out.'

'Could you give me some idea when he's likely to return? I'll call back.'

'I'm afraid I couldn't, Madam. He goes off and there's no knowing when he'll be back. Sometimes he's away for days at a time.'

'It's important,' Phoebe pleaded.

'Yes. I'll tell him,' she promised.

Phoebe hesitated. What else could she say? It seemed so unsatisfactory to leave it like that. That woman's eyes were wandering round the shop, she obviously didn't care a button. The glass bell jangled again as she pulled open the door reluctantly, and an angel from heaven flew into her mind for no reason at all in the shape of the old, old mystery story about the Paris Exhibition and the girl who arrived with her sick mother at the Paris hotel and went out to fetch a doctor and when she returned her mother had disappeared, the room itself had disappeared, and the hotel people swore they had never heard of her or seen her before. And as she recalled this legendary history, she realised intuitively that, if she left the shop without that brooch, when she returned it would no longer be there and they would swear they had never had it. She shut the door of the shop again and advanced with an air of determination to inquire the price.

It was far more money than she was prepared to pay, far more money than it was worth, and she guessed the woman had raised the price because she did not wish to sell. She thought — Wherever possible, be frank, disarm with frankness. And — There is nothing so irresistible as truth.

She dropped the discussion of the price as though suddenly it had ceased to interest her and, touching the brooch lightly with her fingertips, said: 'You know, this belonged to my sister.'

The woman cried: 'We never touch stuff we're not sure of. It was a lady sold it to us!'

Phoebe said: 'But, my dear soul, I never suggested such a thing! My sister has a perfect right to sell her own things if she chooses. Only I've lost touch with her these last few years. As a matter of fact,

I've been abroad, India — ' She owed that much to the Paris Exhibition story, for there the girl and her mother had come from India, where the mother had contracted cholera or the bubonic plague or something that would put paid to the Exhibition if it ever was known, and so cause ruin to thousands of people . . . 'My husband . . . But never mind that: what matters to me now is that I should find my sister. I don't want to go to the police, you can understand that. She might not like it. And then, like a bolt from the blue, I saw this brooch. There couldn't be two alike, could there?'

'I suppose not,' she said reluctantly, not seeing her way.

'What was this lady like; do you remember?'

The woman sought help from the dim ceiling.

'Quiet,' she produced at last, 'and elderly. Biggish, bigger than you, I should say, or perhaps it was her clothes made her look heavier, you know, those loose country sort of tweeds.'

'That's right,' said Phoebe, suddenly

dead sober and afraid, all her mind alert to pick up every hint. 'That sounds like her. Go on.'

'I didn't notice much, really.'

'Can't you give me anything else? That's not much to go on. It might be almost anyone, mightn't it? It sounds like my sister to me, but that may be because I expect it to be her. Can't you remember anything else? Please, try.'

'She had a ring, I think, a signet-ring on her little finger. Did your sister have one?'

'Yes. No. I don't know. She may have.'

'Really nice ring it was. I noticed it, being in the trade. A bloodstone, it was. You don't often see them nowadays.'

'Did she bring in anything else beside the brooch?' She might, after all, have been selling things for Florence if she was a friend, Phoebe supposed.

Yes, she had brought in a job-lot of stuff that she evidently wanted to dispose of. Worthless rubbish most of it, but they had bought the whole lot for the sake of the one good piece. She thought it was last Friday week, but she could look it up for the lady and make certain.

Phoebe wished she would, and she wished that, if it was not too much trouble, the woman would show her the other pieces that the lady-who-might-be-her-sister had brought in. She would buy the brooch in any case, but she might want to buy some of the other things, too.

The woman was gone some time and while she was away Phoebe tried to separate the wheat from the chaff. She thought she could accept the fact that now the woman was telling the truth, whereas before she was lying when she said that the brooch had been bought a long time ago, and her husband had bought it and she knew nothing about it. Clearly, she had been afraid then. And if now she was telling the truth then indeed it did sound as though this ambiguous, unremarkable, middle-aged or elderly lady was the same one who owned a dark green Austin, number YMZ23109. Phoebe rubbed her chilled fingers together. The little shop was cold. Who was this Madam X? And why was she selling Florence's jewellery to an Ol' Clo' shop in a back street of London, when she and Florence had apparently met in Brighton? And where was the connection with Liverpool, where Florence had drawn out her entire savings? And oddly enough, if she was right in her calculations and the woman was right in saying the things had been bought last Friday week, the Liverpool incident came *first*. For it was nearly a week ago that that stupid policeman had told her the Savings Account had been closed out nine days previously, which meant that it was certainly a fortnight ago now. That was surely surpassingly strange. Whatever could Florence need all this money for, and then on top of it to sell her trinkets for the few pounds they would fetch?

Here the woman came in with a bundle and interrupted her train of thought.

'I'd forgotten,' she said. 'There were some old clothes, too. I haven't had time to go through them yet, as you can see.' She untied the string that held them together and spread them out for Phoebe to look at.

She turned them over dully, rather

distastefully, these cheap shabby garments. Who knew where they had come from? This was no use to her. The shoes were looped together with strings pierced through the soft leather. How small they were! A sudden thought blanched her cheek, and she picked up the first garment to hand — a navy stuff frock — and held it up. It would have fitted a child! She pulled out one thing after another with trembling fingers. She remembered giving Florence that little mole-skin tie for her birthday after a good season touring in 'Hayfever'.

Now, she recognized one thing after another.

Meanwhile the woman was wrestling with a knot in the string that fastened a small lumpy packet. With an exclamation of annoyance she cut it and undid the paper.

Phoebe saw a gold link bracelet, a ring with a pale ruby set in gold, a necklace of seed pearls, and a set of false teeth. Without consciously taking in the significance of it, she felt a wave of deadly terror rattle her heart and plant an icy ring, like a cold palm, over her mouth. She could hear the woman talking, but she could not understand a word she was saying, so engrossed was she in the effort not to faint.

She did not faint. But she got out of the place as soon as she could. She thanked the woman appropriately for her trouble, and left a deposit on all the articles she had shown her, for she wanted to make sure that nothing was sold to anyone else yet. Later, if she did not want the stuff herself — But it was not the moment to think of that now. She had the brooch, at least, to prove she had not dreamt it.

Now, first of all, she went back to her flat in St. John's Wood and mixed herself a stiff brandy and soda. She felt miserably numb. She wished she could cry or feel intensely what had happened. Instead, there was nothing but a blank, a dullness, a waiting for something to rouse her feelings to normal reactions once again. For some obscure psychological reason she washed her hands very thoroughly. Then, following an obvious correlation of facts, she changed her dress, cleaned her face and did her hair. She put on a hat, stared at herself in the mirror for a long time, and then took it off again.

Finally, she decided to ring up the Inspector and ask him to come round and see her. Whether he was stupid and inefficient hardly entered into it now, for this was no longer something she could keep to herself.

'I was so glad you rang me up,' Inspector Johnson said when he came round later. 'I wanted to see you. I have news for you. We have traced the car number you gave us.' He paused for effect, and not receiving any — for she looked at him stonily — he hurried on. 'We located it in Liverpool, where it has been sold to a garage-owner there. That seems to tie it up pretty neatly, doesn't it?'

'No.'

The bare monosyllable startled him. And a small laugh flew from his lips. 'Why do you say that?'

'Please sit down. I say 'No' because it doesn't tie up anything.' Phoebe looked at

him with hatred and said slowly: '*After
my sister had closed her post office
account in Liverpool, her jewellery* — her
poor little pieces that passed for jewellery — were sold in London. To a junk
shop off Lamb's Conduit Street, if you
want to be precise. So it isn't very likely
that she sailed for the States, is it?' she
added venomously.

'I don't think we can wash out that
possibility entirely, unless of course you
have proof that she sold the jewellery
herself to this junk shop,' said Inspector
Johnson. If he was cast down by this piece
of enterprise on Phoebe's part and her
chilly manner towards him, he concealed
it very well, and though he had wiped off
his jovial expression, he was as always,
calm and imperturbable.

'On the contrary,' Phoebe assured him,
'I have proof that it was *not* my sister.'
She paused for him to leap in, but he
waited patiently for her to tell him who it
was. 'It was the person — a woman, I
presume, since everyone says she is —
whom I call Madam X for convenience,
but she goes, I believe, by the name of

Mrs. Jolly, and for all I know that may be her real name. Really, I can tell you very little about her,' she said condescendingly, 'beyond the fact that her appearance is unremarkable, that she is elderly and countrified, rents a furnished cottage in a Sussex village called Patchet — incidentally, I think my sister has been there — and owns or did own a dark green Austin, number YMZ23109.'

'I see,' said Inspector Johnson, regarding his nails intently.

'Do you?' said Phoebe with a falsely light tone. 'I wonder.'

What he could not make out was why she was so bitter towards him. Triumph, he would have understood, because she would be thinking herself cleverer than he, or even contempt would have been comprehensible; but not this ill-concealed hatred. He was ashamed of the pain it caused him and knew he was being ridiculous. All the same, he was glad to have seen her own surroundings, at least. These were nice little service flats and this was furnished agreeably with one or two period pieces to lend character.

She tapped a cigarette restlessly on the back of her hand, and he leant forward to light it.

'So you think she has gone off with a woman instead of a man?'

'I think she went off with a woman,' Phoebe agreed quietly.

'Well, that won't make it any more difficult to trace, you know.'

Phoebe looked at him sombrely.

'It's too late,' she said.

'In what way, if you please?'

She said, grimly: 'One sells jewellery, spectacles, all kinds of personal belongings; but would you, in any circumstances whatsoever, sell your false teeth? Even if you have a new denture you keep the old against an emergency, don't you? You couldn't imagine forgetting to put them in in the morning, for instance, could you?'

Inspector Johnson gaped.

'I don't follow. I am sure your reasoning is correct, but I don't see what you are trying to prove.'

'I'm not trying to prove anything: I'm telling you,' Phoebe said sternly. 'With her jewellery, among her clothes, her last pathetic effects, were my poor sister's dentures. I take that to be conclusive.'

He saw now all right. Too late! Oh, too late, indeed! He had not felt so hopelessly inadequate since his prep school days. She had had to face this alone, without warning. He stood up. 'I'm terribly sorry, Mrs. Moore. It must have been a ghastly shock, an unspeakable experience for you. This was a thing I should have been able to prevent. It is useless to apologise now. I have blundered. I feel very badly about it. I must seem very incompetent, very inefficient,' he reproached himself bitterly.

'Oh, what does it matter, now?' Phoebe cried. 'She's dead. I failed her, too. I also am ashamed, I also am not to be forgiven.'

'Oh don't!' said Inspector Johnson. 'You're over-wrought — '

She burst into tears.

'It was so horrible!' she sobbed, suddenly remembering it, feeling it, realizing it in all its poignancy and horror: she had lost her last living relative.

Thus the pain, the shock, the self-reproach and remorse were washed blessedly out of her heart on a flood of tears. She became aware presently that Inspector Johnson was patting her shoulder gently and murmuring vague soothing phrases over the top of her head. She sat up and blew her nose on her handkerchief, which she found conveniently in her hand. She felt exhausted, but calm now and there was no longer room for malice and contempt in her quiet heart. She saw him now as kind and dependable. There is nothing to compare with crying your eyes out on a strange man's handkerchief for founding the basis of a friendship based on confidence and understanding.

Inspector Johnson tactfully went to find her a glass of water while she recovered her equanimity and painted on a new face. He would find something more potent for himself in the corner cupboard, she told him.

He had made a mess of the whole business from beginning to end, in his opinion, and he cursed himself for an incompetent ass. He did not know yet whether he was guilty of criminal negligence, whether if he had been more alert he would have been able to save Florence Brown's life.

What Phoebe wanted to know, of course, was how Florence had died and when? Not to mention where?

The first thing he had to do was to collect the evidence from the junk shop in Lamb's Conduit Street. The second was to go through the lists of registered deaths in England for the last few weeks.

'I shall need to see you again. There are so many questions I shall have to ask you, I'm afraid. But I must return to the station now to put in my report and see to — er — one or two routine matters . . . Would you — would it be frightfully impertinent of me to ask you to have dinner with me tonight? Business, of course,' he added hastily, 'or I shouldn't ask you at such short notice.'

Phoebe pressed her fingertips against her swollen lids thoughtfully.

'Please don't think I'm being hypocritical — it isn't that — I just don't feel like going out this evening. But perhaps you will dine with me here, since, as you say, it is business. I'm quite a handy cook, but if you daren't risk it I'll order the dinner to come up from the restaurant below.'

It was the relief of rain on a dry land to see her smile at him again, naturally.

He went off absurdly elated — his earlier disgrace forgotten — because he was to see her again in a few hours.

3

The Hunt is Up

Over dinner that evening he made her talk about herself, on the pretext of not spoiling the excellent meal with a sad and sordid conversation-matter. She told him, roaming cheerfully from one memory to another, of her husband, her childhood, her career, her dead parents, her relations with her sister, till he had built up some kind of a coherent whole in his mind of her character, outlook, and the way she had struggled against circumstance.

Only afterwards, when the plates had been stacked in the kitchenette and the coffee had boiled and subsided twice, did they begin to talk of more serious matters. He had to tell her that he could not find the registration of Florence's death. She took this as a favourable omen, perhaps signifying that after all she was not dead. He had to disillusion her, to explain that now he must search among the unidentified dead. When she understood she acquiesced sadly. From then on she held back nothing of what she knew. Beginning from the cold grey day of their quarrel and including the attempted suicide, the unanswered 'phone calls and letter, her belated anxiety and her subsequent visits to the caretaker, to the doctor, to Brighton, etc.

He listened attentively and from time to time put a question. He was interested in her visit to Patchet and her conviction that Florence had been to the cottage.

'If she was there she must have been seen by someone,' he averred. 'The point that strikes me chiefly about this story is that they seem so keen never to have been seen together: when Miss Brown is seen she is alone, when Madam X is seen *she* is alone. The only time, so far as we know, that they were seen together was by the page-boy, Jim, and then Madam X was in the car and remained there, presumably unwilling to attract attention. So he never noticed her. She made little enough impression on the people who did see her.

Although, unless people have some good reason to note what a certain person looks like, unless they impress it on their minds in advance that they are going to notice the various details of appearance, it is extremely rare for an untrained observer to carry away anything like an accurate picture of a person. You would hardly credit what discrepancies and deviations there can be in the description of the same person by different witnesses. It is not wise to lend too much value to these vague descriptions of her; both of them seem to have been truly nondescript. Still, we shall make inquiries at Patchet.'

'I can't think who this woman can be,' Phoebe answered obliquely. 'Florence was much too nervous to have picked up with a stranger. And if she knew her before, I never heard of her, and I thought I knew most things about Florence, although she was so secretive, because really there was very little to know, her life was entirely humdrum. But she had a curious character, as different from mine as could be, and I don't think I ever really understood her. She could hold a grievance for years. I'm certain that was why she was so unhappy always; it was her nature to look on the dark side of things and to imagine hatred where only purest love existed.

'I'm not saying she ever had much of a chance in life. And I had a better time than she did and that made her jealous. Nor am I trying to pretend that I was justified in not going away with her when she begged me to. It was beastly of me. I should have realized how much she needed me. But I could not guess that she was going to flounce away in a rage and then work herself into such an insane and suicidal state of mind.

'I understand now why she never answered my 'phone call, nor acknowledged my letter; she was working up a good grudge. No, I'm unjust,' she corrected herself instantly, 'she never received my letter. We are never kind enough, are we?' she said mournfully, switching to another train of thought. 'And the dead remind us bitterly by their absence of lost opportunities.'

She had not much more to tell him and it was growing late, so he took his leave, promising to inform her of any fresh facts.

The first piece of useful evidence that turned up was the discovery of the body. It had been found a few days earlier in Epping Forest by a group of Boy Scouts. It was still wrapped in the soggy remains of two back numbers of *The Times*. (These were later traced with a good deal of trouble to their place of origin — the Brighton Public Library, from where they had evidently been filched. This was mainly useful to the police in showing a possible connection between Brighton and Epping Forest.) The body was in a bad state of preservation: it must have been an unpleasant experience for the Boy Scouts. They did not call Phoebe to identify the body; it would have been useless. Identification was achieved in the surest way possible, by the denture, which corresponded exactly with the gaps among her teeth. But if Phoebe had not come across the false teeth so surprisingly in the junk shop, Florence would have remained forever among the unidentified dead, and she would have been buried wherever they do bury unknown murdered people, and forgotten.

The murderess had covered her tracks carefully and left no other clue to the identity of her victim. If she had dropped the false teeth into the sea, for instance, they would never have been able to connect her with the crime, despite the mishaps that littered her way through no fault of her own; but her cupidity was too much for her, she could not even contemplate throwing away anything which might bring in a few shillings.

At the inquest it was stated that a considerable quantity of Conium, commonly known as Hemlock, was found in the stomach of the deceased. It was judged that the deceased must have absorbed eight or nine grains. The normal dose was from one to three. The sitting was brief and practical. The Coroner directed the jury to their findings, and a verdict was returned of Wilful Murder by Some Person or Persons Unknown. There were few people there, it was totally uninteresting to strangers. Inspector Johnson went down out of curiosity, and on the off-chance of seeing Phoebe.

Immediately after the inquest he contacted the Liverpool police. He wanted to know more in connection with the car, number YMZ23109. What was the name of the previous owner? Did the garage proprietor remember anything about her? Was she looking for another car? That first. Then he wanted them to make further inquiries into the matter of the closed Savings Account of Miss Brown. Did the clerk who had paid over the money remember the appearance of the woman?

The report on the car was at the station when Inspector Johnson arrived the next morning. It was more satisfactory than he had dared hope.

The proprietor remembered the lady quite well; she was a suave, agreeable person, a Southerner by her accent. The name on the driving-license was Mrs. Jolly. He remembered it because he had been amused at the time by its aptness: 'jolly' described her very well. Asked to class her, he suggested that she might be a school matron. She had bought a car in part-exchange for her own, a Morris Oxford, No. QO158249.

So far, so good; that was perfectly satisfactory. Inspector Johnson sent out a call for a Morris Oxford No. QOI58249. Not to be picked up, but located, and if necessary, tailed.

At Liverpool the police were still investigating the business of the closed savings account. It seemed that the post office had been somewhat intrigued — or perhaps alarmed — by their previous query on Miss Florence Brown's behalf and had done a little looking into things on their own account.

Apparently, the signature — the second signature, not the first, the first was all right — on the withdrawal notice was a forgery. So they decided now. Making allowances for the excuse that the woman had made at the time of having a bad hand, there were still obvious characteristics in the second signature which gleamed through the attempted disguise, as different as could be from the signature at the top of the page.

Unfortunately, the post office officials could not describe the woman who had come for the money. Nor could they give the police any help in that direction: the clerk who committed this shocking blunder having been summarily dismissed.

This information they sent down to Inspector Johnson at the St. John's Wood police station, together with a confidential report. And when he had read it he picked up the 'phone and asked the switchboard to get Mrs. Handley, Eskdale Flats, Maida Vale. She was in and answered the 'phone herself. She admitted nervously that she would be at home for the next hour and would see him if he called, for she could think of no suitable excuse. She was torn between curiosity and uneasiness, disliking anything to do with the police, and wondering what on earth he could want to see her about — since he naturally refused to state his business over the telephone.

However, when he came his appearance and manner soon calmed her down, he was so genial and easy. He had come, he explained, in connection with her visit to the Liverpool Police Station some three weeks ago. Did she recall it?

'I'll say I do! I had the most God-awful row with my boyfriend over it when he found out,' Mrs. Handley said frankly. 'Of course I never meant him to know — what the eye doesn't see, the heart doesn't grieve over — but I made some foolish mistake, and he was on to it like a thrush on a snail. He's the jealous type,' she said resignedly, with a sideways glance at the Inspector's manly form. 'We'd already had a bit of an argy-bargy over it, you see, and he didn't want me to do anything about it. No temper was lost or anything, he just advised me to leave it alone. He's like all men; he says — let sleeping dogs lie. Well, there we are, I didn't. I chewed it over, and it somehow seemed wrong not to mention it, and yet at the same time I wasn't surprised that those policemen thought me a bit of a fool; I quite expected them to laugh at me. But now you can tell me was I right or was I wrong?' Her little impudent pug face gazed up at him with what for her was a soulful expression.

'Oh, you were right, of course,' he said hastily. 'It is always wise to report anything that seems to you inexplicable or out of the ordinary. If there's nothing in it, there's no harm done. And you never know; if you don't report it you may be concealing vital information, and perhaps this hesitation allows a criminal to go scot-free because precisely that very piece of evidence is missing. And in connection with your deposition there are just one or two points that I would like to clear up. You say you recognized this person in the post office as a Miss Russell you knew some years ago, but she denied it.'

'Yes, she did at first. She kept saying her name was Brown and she didn't know me from Adam.'

'She said her name was Brown, eh?' he repeated. 'But you were sure she was not telling the truth. You were positive she was this Miss Russell you used to know.'

'Well, I wasn't really,' she said honestly, 'not at the beginning. I just thought it was her as soon as I saw her. I came up behind her and I heard her speaking. I thought I knew her voice — she had a pleasant way of speaking — but it wasn't only that. There is a certain something, I don't know what it is that hangs about people so that you can recognize them at any distance, long before you can distinguish their features. Haven't you noticed? It has always puzzled me. Anyway, you know me, jumping in where angels fear to tread! I never stopped to ask myself whether I was making a mistake, I just bounced right up to her and said 'Wotcher!' or words to that effect.'

'And then?'

'And then she turned round, and of course it didn't look a bit like her. I did feel a fool. Slapping a person on the back and then finding it's a complete stranger. And there were quite a lot of people standing by, too. But then she asked me politely who the hell I thought I was talking to and I wasn't so certain that I had made a mistake; there was her voice and the same haughty way of speaking to me, as though I were dirt. You know, a real lady! Well, anyway, while we were arguing the point I noticed that she had no glove on her right hand and that her first finger was all bandaged up enormous . . . and I saw on her little finger a signet ring that I remembered perfectly well. So that was that, wasn't it?' she smiled. 'I saw she didn't want to acknowledge me for some reason or another, so I made myself scarce. But I kept my eyes open and I can see out of the back of my head as well as the next man.'

'Just one moment,' said the Inspector. 'You say it didn't look like her when she turned round. In what way?'

'She looked younger, and harder, in a way that I couldn't place at first. I know the word I want: she looked too *modern*. She had on a turban, and high heels and all that. She wasn't the type. She looked like a parson's wife when I knew her. She wore the same old things from one year's end to another; didn't know the first thing about clothes.'

'Yes, I see. Please go on.'

'Where was I? Oh yes, in the post office . . . Well, I walked down the street and waited for her to come out. No, no, I'm forgetting. I daresay I wouldn't have bothered anymore, but I saw the girl behind the counter hand her a great wedge of notes — I've never seen such a quantity in all my life! Well, of course I couldn't help wondering a bit about it, it's only human nature, isn't it? So when she came out at last I had another shot. She still wouldn't admit she knew me, and at last she roused my paddy and I told her that it wasn't a bit of use her lying, because I'd recognized her ring. I marched off then. I let her see I was in a huff. She came running after me, of course, and I must say she looked as if I'd given her a bit of a turn. Well, she said she could explain everything, and we went off to a teashop to have a little chat. I was dying of curiosity by now. Why all the secrecy? I thought. I guessed there was a man behind it. There always is with a woman. And she said there was and she was sailing to America the next day. Well, all right, I thought, there's nothing much wrong with that for a story, except that she still seems a trifle close. We still weren't exactly girls together, though we were pretending to be. I could think of plenty of reasons for her to have changed her name and to be reserved about her movements. She wouldn't be the first woman to be doing a bunk with a married man, for instance. I've done it myself,' she said, with a funny mixture of archness and pride, running her fingers through her yellow hair. 'But where it all went queer to me was when I discovered that her eyes were made of brown glass!'

'These contact lenses, you mean. You suddenly noticed them, and that was what alarmed you.'

'Yes. That was what made her look so different, of course. It was horrid!'

'You didn't mention it to her?'

'No. I kind of felt instinctively that there was some phonus-bolonus about the whole business. It made me feel quite dickey, and all I wanted to do was get away. Only, thinking it over afterwards, it seemed to me that I'd been a bit of a wet fish. I ought to have had more guts. I should have found out more about her. I thought if she was a wrong 'un the police would probably be wild with me for letting her go so easily.'

'But though it may seem unusual, there's nothing really wrong in wearing brown lenses, even if you have got blue eyes. You must have had more than that to go on,' Inspector Johnson said.

'There was the business of the cat. I suppose I never really forgot that.' Mrs. Handley — as she called herself now — stirred the cold black coffee in her cup absently. She glanced nervously at the policeman. But he was sitting calmly still, as if all eternity lay before him in a shining sea so that he might listen to all the secrets of the universe. 'That happened just before we left Christbourne. 'The place that God forgot,' my hubby used to call it. Anyway, this Miss Russell lived next door with her old father. I can't say we were very friendly. But I did my best because I was sorry for her; I've seen lives wasted like that before with selfish parents, and it makes me mad. But, as I say, it never came to anything because she thought herself too good, too much of a lady, to have much to do with people like Sid and me.

'But of course the night her Dad died and she was all alone in the house it was only natural that she should run over to us. And I went back with her. And while she was upstairs with the doctor, I saw the cat. It was lying on the draining-board, as dead as mutton. A lovely little Persian, he was, and she adored him — you know, a real old maid. But he wasn't lovely then, he looked dreadful. Well, I thought, there's a perfectly young and healthy cat kicked the bucket. Why? He must have eaten something that disagreed with him. And then I thought, he and the old man must have died about the same time, and it seemed such a nasty coincidence, I didn't like it. I went home. I don't know what happened. She never said anything to me. But sometime after, I said casually that I hadn't seen Pussy anywhere for ages, and she said No, that he must have run away or been stolen. Well, I knew she couldn't really believe that, so she must have been lying to me. For some reason, she didn't want me to know that Pussy was dead, had died the same night as her father. Well, there wasn't anything I could do about it, so I put it out of my head.'

'I'm still not quite clear what you think happened to the cat?' said Inspector Johnson patiently.

'Oh, I'm willing to admit that I may be wasting your time and imagining things. It was really more of a *feeling* than anything else. That's why I was so reluctant to go to the police, because I had so few what you'd call facts.'

'But all the same, you had this feeling which persisted over a number of years, so it must have been fairly strong,' he urged her gently back on to the line of thought. 'What was it now?'

'I'll tell you. I reasoned like this.' She ticked them off on her fingers as she enumerated them. 'If Pussy was poisoned it was either on purpose or by accident. If it was on purpose it may have been because he was the only medium she had to hand for experimenting on. If it was accident he must somehow have got hold of some and food or liquid intended for someone else. There were only three people in that house; herself, her father and the nurse. She was alive; the nurse was out; her father died. It seems pretty obvious. She must have been fed up to the teeth looking after that pernickety old fellow for years, without anything to look forward to. I bet she felt that if he was ill enough to have a nurse in the house no one would be very surprised if he died. Besides, he was over eighty, you know.'

'The doctor signed the death certificate without any fuss?'

She nodded.

'It wouldn't be the first time that had happened, would it?'

'Did she inherit a great deal from him? Did she radically alter her mode of living after his death?'

But there Mrs. Handley's usefulness failed him: they had left Christbourne shortly after. He put a few more questions, about dates and times mostly, and then took his leave.

There were still not many firms in England that made contact lenses and routine inquiries soon elicited the desired information about the pair tinted brown that were sold to a woman between the tenth and fifteenth of the month. Inspector Johnson realised with pleasure that it was not a coincidence but a link in the chain of evidence connecting the two women, that Madam X had bought them from the firm where Miss Brown had worked for twenty years.

The car was located by the Cornwall police at Falmouth, where Madam X was residing for the present.

Phoebe, who was kept up to date as far as possible with the fresh facts, when told of this last development expostulated irritably.

What were the police waiting for? They had her under their hand, all they had to do was to pick her up. Why were they holding back? What more did they want? Were they always so reluctant to make an arrest?

Inspector Johnson pointed out to her patiently that while they had her under their hand they need not hurry or worry themselves, they could pick her up at any time. Meanwhile, they were collecting evidence. They had by no means sifted all the possible factors. As for arresting the woman, they really had nothing to arrest her on. There was nothing in the least conclusive about the evidence they had acquired up to the present. And the circumstantial evidence was really of the slightest. Suppose they arrested her now and made the charge a heavy one. Then, the evidence proving insufficient, she would almost certainly be released before they could gather fresh and more important facts, and then they would be in the soup indeed. The personal liberty of the subject was a serious matter in England. She might sue them for unlawful detention, if she pleased. Again, if they merely pulled her in on a light charge and she was released, as she would be, the only purpose that had served was to put her on her guard. As it was, the mouse ran in and out of its hole unperturbed, while the cat watched placidly from a distance, certain that she had but to raise her paw to stop the mouse's little games forever.

And if the mouse should run away?

Inspector Johnson smiled at Phoebe's

question, and promised her that he would not allow that to happen.

She supposed crossly that she would have to trust him, since there was nothing else she could do. Although she had not much confidence in the police generally, she was beginning to believe him reliable. He was so equable, she had never seen him out of humour except for the one sad occasion when he had been ashamed of himself because she had had to tell him he had failed and Florence was dead. She liked his quiet wisdom, his patience, his understanding of human nature. He was not exciting or adventurous, but then did one want those qualities in a man? It depended, she reproved her thoughts sharply, what one wanted the man for.

As for the Inspector, he of course could not speak, was determined not to open his mouth until this business was safely concluded. He would only make a fool of himself if he did, he knew. Besides, there was no need to hurry. It was funny how when you were young you could not bear to have to wait an instant for anything you really wanted, but when you grew older, even though you knew you had not much more time, nothing seemed so pressing.

Despite his day-dreams, he managed to get his work done. Following the thread backwards from the end to the beginning, as he hoped, he was at present checking up on the events at Patchet. There was an enterprising young sergeant of the local police there and he went at it with a will. He examined the cottage very thoroughly, with no practical results save reward of one magnificent fingerprint, or rather — hand-print, which he found on the table in the small bedroom. He was pleased with his trophy and not the least disheartened that he had found nothing else. The significance of the mirror turned to the wall, of course, he could not be expected to see. But that did not matter, because Phoebe had gathered that, as well as the cigarette end in the flower bed . . .

As far as he could make out the supposed tenant or tenants of the cottage could not have been there longer than a week. Even so, in that time someone must have seen them. The trades-people recalled vaguely this middle-aged lady who drove up in a car to get her groceries and meat, or to have her car filled at the little garage on the corner of the High Street. But so far as they could remember she was always alone. Who would have called at the house, apart from the trades-people? No villagers paid much attention to casual visitors as a rule, they were all too concerned with their own affairs to, be interested in 'foreigners.' But the vicar's wife was very dutiful, almost excessively so, thought the young sergeant with a wry grin, and she might have called. At any rate, she would not be offended if he asked her.

Yes, she had called, just the once, she remembered when asked, for the lady — what was her name now? Mrs. Gay, or something like that — anyway, she had not been very forthcoming. She seemed very agreeable. Oh yes, quite pleased to see her. What had she said now? The vicar's wife smote her forehead in despair at her failing memory. Oh yes, that she was looking for a small house in the district for herself and her son. No, she didn't think the son was there with her, she rather thought Mrs. Gay, or whatever her name was, had said she was there alone. But it was funny that Sergeant Hoskins should mention that, because she remembered now something that had rather puzzled her at the time: the lady had left the room for something and she could have sworn that she heard her talking to someone. Now wasn't that odd?

Here, the vicar's wife, almost bursting with curiosity, offered to treat in the strictest confidence anything Sergeant Hoskins cared to tell her of what had happened to the strange lady. The sergeant was polite and discreet: unfortunately he wasn't in a position to tell the vicar's wife anything, because he knew nothing himself and was merely detailed to make some routine inquiries.

Well, that was that. It might be interesting to find out if any 'phone calls had been put through for that period, if she had any contact with the outside world it could not but be helpful to know with whom. Automatic dialling had not yet come to Patchet, so it was not difficult to trace calls incoming and outgoing at the telephone exchange.

Miss Garrett at the exchange repeated to him in awestruck tones the two words she had heard gasped from that number on the night of the 12th. She vowed she would never forget the peculiar horror of the silence that followed. She had, of course, rung Dr. Benson and advised him of what had taken place, leaving it to his discretion to go or not.

So Sergeant Hoskins paid a visit to Dr. Benson after surgery hours . . .

'The night of the 12th,' mused Dr. Benson, flicking through his file of notes with a frown. 'Oh yes, the lady at Ivy Cottage. A funny case. Called me out in the middle of the night. Nothing wrong with her that I could see. Nerves, I expect. Though, to be fair, she didn't look neurotic. Told her to come down to the surgery next day to be examined, but she never turned up. Got the wind up about something, I suppose. Women of that age . . . Took the trouble to drive up and see she was all right the day after and got no answer. Rang and rang. The place looked as if it was shut up. People like that deserve to be scragged. No consideration.'

Sergeant Hoskins had some difficulty in following this, and asked the doctor to tell him as accurately as possible what had occurred from the beginning.

'The exchange rang you and told you that they believed you were wanted urgently at Ivy Cottage, wasn't that it?'

'Yes. I thought it might be a practical joke. It has been known. Still, can't take chances like that. Went down there, as I told you. Place in darkness. Knocked and rang. No answer. I could hear a dog yapping inside, a sound like chips of ice flying through the air. In the end the woman came and let me in. Seemed a bit surprised, I thought, or a bit slow in the uptake. Didn't seem able to make out what it was all about. 'Someone sent for me,' I said. 'Can I see the patient?' 'I'm the patient,' says she. I asked her what the trouble was and she hummed and hawed and said it was nothing at all and she was all right now. She didn't seem anxious for me to look at her, but of course I did. Her pulse was a bit rapid but perfectly strong. I thought she looked a bit green about the gills. Told me she'd fainted for the first time in her life. Forgivable panic in a woman living alone, as she told me she was.

'Sat and talked for a bit, to make her feel at ease. Psychology.' He laughed suddenly. 'I remember there was a dickens of a row going on upstairs. 'Birds,' says she, 'in the rafters.' I'm country bred, Sergeant. If those were birds in the rafters, then I've got bats in my belfry. I offered to go up and have a look round for her. But she wasn't having any. Funny lady, eh? Not my place to interfere if there was anything shady going on. For all I knew her gentleman friend might be paying her a late call. I rather inclined to that view. Accounted for her unwillingness to let me in, in the first instance. Or she might have a drunken husband. Perhaps he frightened her and she rang up for help and then was ashamed to let him down by admitting it. Only suggestions, of course. I left then. Nothing more to tell you.'

Asked to describe her, he gave a better account than most.

She was, he thought, in the region of fifty-five, well-preserved, and sturdy. Weighed about eleven stone, and was about five foot seven in height. Florid complexion, white hair, blue eyes, a rather thin mouth and small well-shaped teeth.

Oh yes, there *was* a dog, a little black Cairn.

A new and puzzling factor entered in with the identification of the hand-print. For one thing, the sergeant had not much hope that it would be identified, presuming it to belong to one or other of the two women in question and he did not believe that either of them was likely to prove known criminals. Now it appeared that the print was of one Slimy Joe, a well-known prig and house-breaker. A startling new development indeed, as the journalists say. He'd been convicted several times, and though he never spent long in jail, for his offences were not serious, he was never outside for very long. He was a hopeless and unpleasant type, but not dangerous. Like all criminals, he never ventured beyond his own line. He could not be imagined as a murderer even under provocation. On the contrary he could be more readily visualized as a murderer. Yet was it not more than a coincidence that his prints should be there?

'Here's a rum go!' said Inspector Johnson, and sent out a call for Slimy Joe to be picked up wherever he was.

Meanwhile, Sergeant Hoskins had been questioning the local grocer's delivery-boy on a personal matter unconnected with his work — a little affair of a broken window, of which he was suspected to have some knowledge. And by the merest fluke, Hoskins, remembering his job, asked him if he had had occasion to call recently at Ivy Cottage.

He admitted that he had. He admitted that he had seen a lady there. Small and dark, she was, and she looked sort of cross and frightened. She'd made a fuss about paying for the goods and he'd had to pretend he was going to take them away again, because Mr. Blaine, his boss, didn't like him to leave things without the money when they didn't know the people. She'd paid up in the end, of course. Mr. Blaine said they always did, it was just a try-on.

And she was small and dark, he was quite sure about that? He was positive, he asserted. Would he recognize her if he saw her again, would he know her from a photograph? He thought he would.

Sergeant Hoskins glowed. He'd done a good bit of work, no doubt about it. He had at last established a connection between the two women. If they had not been seen together, they had at least definitely been in the same house together at approximately the same time.

4

The Pace Quickens

Phoebe was becoming impatient. This hanging about alarmed her. She was not entirely convinced that the police had everything under control. She trusted Inspector Johnson as a man, but how efficient was he as a policeman? That was the question that bothered her. And it by no means only depended on him. It was all very well to say they had their eye on Madam X, but she could easily slip away. One of these days the policeman would close his eyes in a yawn and when he opened them again she would be gone. That would be a pretty kettle of fish, wouldn't it? While they pottered about questioning people who had no memories and used neither their eyes nor their ears. Where did they hope to get by doing that? Collecting evidence, was it? What did they think they would achieve thereby? Why, in the name of goodness, didn't they do something positive? Why couldn't they force the issue a bit? 'If you haven't enough evidence, invent it,' Phoebe argued, full of the pioneer spirit. 'Do something, don't wait for the woman to throw herself into your arms. That is, if you're sure she is the guilty person. If you're not sure, make sure.'

It seemed so ludicrously clear and simple to her. Men pottered about and made generalizations and insisted that everything should be done according to rule. Women simply went and did the thing and got it over. Good heavens, she supposed they would say it was bad form to try and get hold of a dangerous criminal by laying a trap for her. And yet it seemed the most obvious thing in the world to dangle a decoy in front of the woman and see what she did. That was what she would do if she had her way . . . Why not, indeed? She was of age and free to do as she liked. It was certainly her concern. She knew more or less where to find her. Inspector Johnson had told her some time back that she was in Cornwall, at a place called Falmouth. It might not be easy to find a nondescript middle-aged lady, with no further means of identification beyond a ring, a car number, and a little dog. And for all Phoebe knew, she might have none of those things now, any more than it was to be presumed that she was still called Mrs. Jolly.

Of course Phoebe could go to the Falmouth police and ask them to point out to her the woman they were watching on instructions from London. Inspector Johnson could provide her with credentials so that they should not doubt her word or her identity.

Yes, but was that wise? She could imagine Inspector Johnson fussing like a flustered mother-hen at any attempt to interfere with the sacred routine — a woman, and a lay-woman at that, mark you! He would surely die. Besides, it would be tactless to suggest that she thought them so incompetent that she had come to do their work for them, to show them how it should be done, to offer them a helping hand — oh, in the friendliest spirit, of course! She could imagine how they would welcome it.

She grimaced. No, it would never do. Even in this day and age it was still necessary for a woman to pretend to believe in the old myth of man's superiority. If she was to carry this through she would have to do it alone and they must be told nothing about it. She had little doubt that she could handle this situation better than any mere policeman. It took a woman to understand feminine psychology. Surely that was obvious to the meanest mind.

Perhaps she wasn't playing quite fair. But if she let him know what she intended to do he would most certainly prevent her. That he must not do. A smile involuntarily curved her full lips upward. She would leave him a clue; the rest was up to him. She would have done her bit, and perhaps it was better to be on the safe side, then he would have nothing to reproach her with after. And if he didn't 'get it,' well, that only showed he was a pretty poor policeman.

Then how was she to find this woman among a crowd of several thousand people? She might never see her. And how was she to attract this one woman into her hands?

She decided finally to risk an advertisement in a local paper; and she spent some time concocting a suggestive snare. The advertisement appeared the following week in *The Cornish Weekly Gazette* in the Personal column and read thus:

LONELY: An agreeable companion wanted for a few months for lady without friends in England. Apply Royal Hotel, Falmouth, between ten and eleven in the morning, after Tuesday next.

A lonely lady, presumably a foreigner since she did not live in England, and who was staying at the most expensive hotel in the place, should prove an attractive bait, Phoebe thought. It ought to stimulate some result.

The day the newspaper came out Phoebe travelled down to Cornwall, wearing her most discreet and expensive black. Before she left, however, she suffered a pang of guilt about her behaviour towards Inspector Johnson. He might not think it clever; he might not be amused. Perhaps she wasn't playing quite fair. She would leave him a clue; the rest was up to him. In her careless flowing script she scrawled a few words on a postcard and addressed it to the St. John's Wood Police Station. She dropped it in the pillar box with a chuckle.

She took an imposing suite on the first floor of the Royal Hotel. It was going to run into a lot more money than she could afford, but to hell with expense, she thought. Toasted cheese had a more alluring odour to mice than the ordinary kind . . . and so even if Phoebe had no money to speak of, an aroma of affluence would be sure to attract this particular mouse towards the trap. And once this particular mouse had smelt the cheese she would know what to do. She had the bare bones of a plot in her mind; nothing too rigid or stereotyped; she believed in trusting to the inspiration of events.

Phoebe was passing as the widow of a South African diamond merchant, who, having no family of her own, had returned for a period of time to her native land. But, she complained, she did not care for England anymore; the climate was disagreeable, the natives unfriendly, the atmosphere banal to a degree; in short, it was as unlike Durban as possible. The lady was bored. And she was difficult to please. Not one of all the possible companions who offered their services — and it was surprising how many there were, for some had come from far away — was just what she wanted. This one was too young, that one too old. This one too acquiescent, that one too inclined to bully. She was not difficult, she was not disagreeable, she protested, what she wanted really was a friend.

There were plenty of gentlemen in the hotel who would have been only too pleased to show the lady a little friendliness. But she was still in mourning for her dear husband, besides she was not interested in that sort of friendship. She was difficult, she was disagreeable with those gentlemen, perforce. For it would not do at all if they took to following her about and watching what she did, where she went and to whom she spoke.

Mrs. Leah Abrams was cold, melancholy, took most of her meals alone in her room, and between whiles frequented the busiest spots in the town, watching the passers-by, from café or promenade, with an air of concentration; her long fingers absently crumbling a roll perhaps while her restless eyes flickered over the cars crawling up and down the street. But never did she see one marked QO158249.

The third day, when she was beginning to feel a bit of a fool already, there were more applicants than hitherto to choose from. She did not need to waste any time with the younger ones, only people obviously over forty did she consider. There were three in that category. One could only come for three hours a day as she had to look after an invalid sister. That would not be Madam X, for she would not acknowledge any ties, besides she was much too small and thin to be possible. The next was obviously a born companion, with all her bona fides in her hand, as it were; references from Lady

This and the Honourable Mrs. That, and a whole spate of what she expected in the way of work and the benefits she was accustomed to. Phoebe soon got rid of her. The interviewing period was nearly up, there was just time for one more.

Phoebe stiffened imperceptibly as she came in; this one was the likeliest yet, so far as appearance went: thick-set, large-boned, dressed in good plain tweeds. A woman who might be any age between forty-five and sixty, with soft becoming white hair, a bonny complexion and a frank blue eye that met yours fair and square. Phoebe, who considered herself no mean judge of character, thought — Oh no, impossible! This woman could never do anything underhand, you've only to look at her.

'Do sit down,' said Phoebe in her silkiest voice. 'Now, let me see . . . what is your name? I've got the cards muddled up, I think.'

'Miss Lowell — Eleanor Lowell. I called yesterday, as a matter of fact, but I was too late, you had already left.'

'What a nuisance! I'm so sorry. Did

you have far to come?'

'No,' said Miss Lowell, with charm but resolution.

'Do take off your coat, it's so warm in here.'

Phoebe prattled fertilely about herself and her dear husband and how much she missed him now that he had left her alone in the world, while she narrowly watched Miss Lowell remove first one glove and then the other, preparatory to taking off her coat. She had nice hands, large, bare and ringless. Phoebe felt a wave of relief and disappointment at the same time. But almost in the same instant her quick eyes noticed that the little finger of her right hand was pinched in at the base where the flesh had been recently constricted by the pressure of a band. Then, she *had* worn a ring on that finger, constantly and for a long time. Not that that proved anything.

Mrs. Abrams murmured about references.

Miss Lowell gazed at her frankly.

'I'll be perfectly honest with you, there's no point in being otherwise or in beating about the bush. I'm not a companion. I never have been. And I hope to God I never shall be.' She smiled humorously. 'I misread your advertisement. I didn't know you meant that kind of a companion, I thought you meant someone to be friendly with more than anything else.'

'But I did, I did,' exclaimed Phoebe. 'How clever of you to guess, when all the others thought . . . '

Miss Lowell, who had carefully inquired her chances before entering the race, looked pleased.

'I know what it's like to be lonely, though I haven't the experience of being alone in a strange land, thank goodness. Still, I'm lonely now. I retired a few months ago. And it's so dull, I don't know what to do with myself. I taught school for thirty years. Now it's all playtime and I've forgotten how.'

'Then you too were looking for someone with whom to go about and share expenses, is that it?'

Miss Lowell eyed Phoebe, languid in superb black chiffon with something that sparkled at the throat and her audacious hair hidden beneath a black and white silk scarf, dubiously.

'I don't know . . . ' she said hesitantly, and blushed. 'I'm not exactly well off. I probably couldn't afford . . . '

'I should consider it my privilege,' Phoebe said graciously.

'Oh! Would that be quite fair?' You could see Miss Lowell was painfully honest. Phoebe said with pitiful melancholy:

'My dear, what am I to do with all my money? I can't take it with me, and I've no one to leave it to. It's little enough to do in return for friendship.'

She explained that she had friends in South Africa, of course, but what use was that to her here, when the doctors had insisted that she return to live for six months of the year at least in the cooler climate of England. Her health? Here Phoebe laughed with forced gaiety. She was perfectly all right really. She didn't require nursing if that was what Miss Lowell was afraid of. Well, if she must know, the doctors said she had something

that they called 'tropical heart.' Dangerous? She hoped not.

Dangerous, presumably, if she had
remained in her home abroad. And she
had really been wondering these last few
days whether it might not be better to die
abruptly of 'tropical heart' than to creep
on into a lonely old age and die of
boredom. She had seriously considered
buying herself a pet, a little dog, for
company and affection. Was Miss Lowell
fond of animals? Miss Lowell had a little
dog, a Cairn bitch named Belinda. A
friendly little soul. Mrs. Abrams would be
sure to love her. Mrs. Abrams agreed
enthusiastically that she was sure she
would.

Further details were discussed. Presently Phoebe remarked that if anything
came of this and they did join forces it
would be nice for them to have a car to go
about in. The Daimler Hire people were
very good, she believed.

Miss Lowell, staring out of the window
at the tossing blue sea, made no reply.

Did not Miss Lowell agree?

Miss Lowell shook herself like a dog

coming out of water and blinked.

'I'm sorry. I was thinking of something else. A car, you say? I have a car. Nothing very grand. But I'd be pleased to put it at your disposal. It's good enough for trundling along these roads.'

There were one or two more points to be gone into and then they decided to think the matter over for a day and then communicate their decision to one another the day after. They would meet at such and such a café for tea. They shook hands, and Miss Lowell went away, leaving Phoebe with much food for thought.

Adding up the facts one way it seemed glaringly plain that this Miss Lowell as she called herself was the very person Phoebe was looking for. The build and type and age all fitted; she had a car and a dog, and she had been accustomed to wear a ring on the little finger of her right hand. She was alone and a free agent.

On the other hand, Phoebe simply could not visualize her as a murderess. It was impossible. She was too forthright, too nice. She was surely telling nothing but the truth when she said she was a school-teacher, she had all the broad outlook, the firmness and assurance of one. That was far easier to believe than that she had got hold of some defenceless stupid woman and killed her for gain. You simply could not see Miss Lowell in that role at all. Did anyone mean to tell her that Miss Lowell was such a consummate actress that she could put all that on? Because if they did, she would simply refuse to believe it. She knew something of the art herself, and it was one thing to pretend to be the wife of a South African millionaire when you'd never been nearer South Africa than a Jaffa orange; but quite another to disguise one's true characteristics, the furtive eye, the twitching finger, the nervous glance over one's shoulder for the footsteps padding behind; all these which must surely be inherent in the craft of murder were less easy to obviate and supplant with a relaxed pose, a smiling ingenuous face, breathing good-temper and a contented mind.

Perhaps she was wasting time and

money in chasing this shadow. Should she drop it, return to town defeated, and leave it to the police to manage as best they could? Wasn't it rather absurd for her to imagine for an instant that she could succeed where they so far had failed? It seemed to her now, in this doubtful frame of mind, that there was more than a touch of megalomania in her attitude. If she went ignominiously back to London, no one need ever know. If Inspector Johnson suspected, it could remain but a suspicion.

But at three o'clock she woke with a start and thought of Florence. After all, that was why she was here really. What did it matter whether she made a fool of herself or not. She was out to pay part of the debt she owed to her sister. She was a soft, vain, egotistical fool, but that much she would do.

She was inclined to trust Miss Lowell. She had taken a fancy to her. But if her car number turned out to be QO158249, she would not hesitate to follow it through to the bitter end.

There was also the possibility to be

considered that at most she was an accomplice and that there was someone else, someone not touched on as yet, who had performed the actual crime. So Phoebe hoped the next day when she met Miss Lowell as arranged and saw her step out of a dull red Morris Oxford, with the number — yes, the number she had dreaded but expected to see. She felt suddenly immensely weary, as though she had assumed a burden too great for her to manage, as though she had seen through all the goodness in the world to a little flickering core of evil, as though nastiness and cruelty lay eternally behind the smiling surface of innocence.

It required all her courage and acting ability to behave naturally and graciously as befitted her role of wealthy matron. While she talked lightly of the scene before them, her thoughts were with her dead sister and she wondered what ruse this woman had employed; how had she coaxed that nervous little creature to her side, how induced her to stay there? And had Florence trusted her to the end? Did she never know what had happened?

Looking at that amiable face and remembering the poor little crumpled corpse, treated with such ignominy, Phoebe shuddered with a sudden impulse of fear. Here lay danger.

While Phoebe was going through this wretched state of indecision, the Hull police had picked up Slimy Joe in a casual ward and lugged him off to the station to be questioned.

Slimy Joe was irate with anxiety. What were they going to pin on him this time? He knew the police and their nasty little games — or so he maintained. He had no illusions about the way they 'cooked' evidence. Hadn't he been 'framed' time and time again himself? He'd never had a fair deal. 'Justice isn't for poor swine like us,' he often cried with lamentable cynicism.

Inspector Turnbull — familiarly known as the Horror of Hull — greeted him genially.

'Well, well, Slimy, it's nice of you to call. You wanted to have a little chat with us, eh?'

'Not me, I didn't,' said Slimy truthfully.

'It wouldn't break *my* heart if I never saw your ugly mug again.'

'You disappoint me, Slimy. Your manners don't improve, nor do you grow any wiser.'

'Let's skip all the lah-di-dah. I've got an important engagement in an hour's time — with the Dook of Windsor, if you want to know, and it won't do to keep 'is Royal 'ighness waiting.'

'We only want to know what you've been doing with yourself lately, Slimy.'

'I'm on the road. The doctor says I've got consumption and I need an open air life,' he said proudly. 'And plenty of nourishing stout. Yus, you've got nothing on me this time. I'm going straight now.'

'I'm not talking about the last five minutes. I know you're straight *now* because I've got you under my eye,' said the genial inspector.

'Oh, very sourcastic, ain't we! I've been on the road for the last two months, anyway. You ask anyone you like an' they'll tell you I'm straight now. Everyone sees me going up and down. An' I meet a lot of coves from the old days in the casuals.'

'Do you always sleep in casuals?'

'Not if it's fine. I doss under a hedge or against a rick.'

'I can just see you,' said the inspector demurely.

'I do,' said Slimy indignantly. 'Cor stone me, ain't that a ruddy split all over. 'E won't believe you when you do tell 'im the truth.'

'God forbid I should doubt your integrity in any way. What route have you been following this last month, then? Just to give me an idea.'

'I've been — ' Slimy opened his mouth and closed it again with an air of finality.

'Forgotten?' suggested Inspector Turnbull.

Slimy shrugged.

'Can't say I was paying any attention. Course, if I'd of known you was going to take a personal interest in me eyetinery I'd of kept a diary.'

'Well, yes, it is a good idea to keep a diary. It makes an alibi of sorts, you know.'

'Alibi?' said Slimy, glancing quickly right and left from the corners of his eyes.

'Sleeping under a hedge isn't much of an alibi, unless you had some tramping pal with you.'

'I don't 'ave to bother me 'ead about that nowadays. I'm straight, see!'

'Where were you on the night of the 12th?' he said sharply, suddenly thrusting his face almost into Slimy Joe's.

''Ere, you're not going to try and pin anything on me, are you?' he whined. ''Ow can I remember where I was on the 12th. Why should I? I ain't done nothing wrong. If we try to go straight you don't give us a chance. Got a bit of work hanging lose that you want to clear up: 'stick it on any one. Who 'aven't we 'ad in lately? Well, pull 'im in for a change, 'e'll do.'

The inspector yawned ostentatiously.

'Get on to the alibi, Slimy, do. I thought you had an important engagement.'

'Alibi!' shrieked Slimy. 'I ain't got an alibi. I don't need one. I keep telling you I ain't touched a job for more'n two months. That's the bleeding truth and God's my witness.'

Inspector Turnbull wiped the patient smile off his face and looked deadly serious. He tapped the papers on the desk before him with the back of his nails.

'You say you haven't done a 'job' for over two months, but I have definite information . . .'

Slimy wrung his hands histrionically.

'Some busy's got his needle in me. What do they say? I ain't done a thing. Ain't it cruel!'

The inspector said quietly: 'You were seen in Patchet.'

'Never been there in me life! Never heard of the place before! It's a lie, and whoever told you was a liar!' he exclaimed with mechanical vigour, but you could tell from the flurried glances he sent to the ceiling, as though his memory was printed there in invisible ink, that he was trying to remember, trying hastily to collect his wits.

Inspector Turnbull simulated mild astonishment.

'But you must have come through

Patchet today. It's on the left as you enter Hull from the North Road.'

The thin blue veins on the tramp's forehead subsided.

'I didn't come in that way,' he said. 'I thought you meant . . . '

'You thought I meant Patchet under the Sussex Downs. Yes, Slimy, I did. And if you weren't there that night, where were you?' He leant forward with terrifying good humour.

'What night? Where? Oh, Gawd, you're trying to 'frame' me!' stuttered Slimy. 'I don't know what you're talking about. What night?'

'The night you broke into Ivy Cottage. Remember?'

'I never did. I never was anywhere near there. If I was seen, it's a lie, or it's some bloke that looks like me.'

'Won't do.'

'Tell me when it was and maybe I can remember what I was doing just then. I daresay I was the other side of the country.'

'Won't do. You left your fingerprints behind you. Very thoughtful and we're much obliged. Now explain how they came there.'

Slimy went an ugly greenish-white under the eyes. He was silent a moment, plucking his under lip with a choppy finger.

'It was empty,' he said, 'the house was empty. And it was a dirty night. It wasn't going to do any harm if I got in. I only wanted to keep dry. The doctor said if I got another dose of fever I'd be done for. I gotta be careful, see.'

'Yes, you've got to be careful,' the inspector agreed ominously. 'Yes, I see. And you spent the night there?'

'I never said that. S'matter of fact, I didn't. Something disturbed me. I got scared and did a bunk.'

'Now, whatever could have scared a great tough chap like you? You wouldn't be afraid of mice, or ghosts. It couldn't be anything like that. More likely to be a person.'

Slimy said almost eagerly:

'Yus. All of a sudden I thought I heard someone coming in. The owner, p'haps. I wasn't taking any chances, anyway. I got out of the window as quick as you like, and shinned down the drain-pipe.'

'You were upstairs, then?'

'I ran upstairs when I heard them coming.'

'And she ran after you, eh?'

'She?' Fear spread over Slimy's face like a grey witness. 'I never said it was a she.'

'No. I said it,' said the inspector pleasantly. 'Then she ran after you,' he repeated. 'She called to you to stop, perhaps. You turned round and threatened her, just to keep her quiet, eh? You never meant to harm her, of course. And it must have given you a nasty turn when you realized she was dead. I daresay your one idea then was to get as far away as possible, but you weren't in too much of a hurry to pick up a few useful little pieces, were you? If you yell like that, Slimy, I'll have you locked up straight away. Shut up!'

But Slimy's nerves were out of control. He was a sick man. The shrieks came out of his mouth despite himself. He was not even aware that he was making that shrill and tortured noise. A constable obligingly threw a glassful of cold water into his face, and pushed a chair under his knees.

He sank into it, trembling and shuddering like a frightened horse. He sat there panting, and presently pulled a dirty rag out of his pocket and wiped off the water still running down his face.

'Take your time,' said the inspector kindly.

Slimy groaned heavily and mumbled to himself.

'I'm for it now,' he said in a low voice. 'I reckon I'm done for. I'm as innocent as a new-born lamb this time, but the cops'll never believe that. I never laid a finger on her. She was dead afore ever I saw her.'

'Begin from the beginning, Slimy.' Inspector Turnbull raised a finger to the constable by the door, who brought out his shorthand pad and licked his pencil.

Slimy scratched his head vigorously to restore the circulation.

'I'd noticed the dump a few days before when I was in them parts,' he began hoarsely. 'I allus notice the empty houses, you never know when they're going to be useful. And this one was still furnished.

There's no harm that I can see in sleeping on a proper bed, by way of a change, even if it don't belong to you.'

'Stick to the truth,' warned the inspector abstractedly.

Slimy sighed and gazed at him yearningly.

'All right. It looked like a soft crib. So when I was ready I came back, see? Wasn't it just my mucking luck that that happened to be the very night — ' he broke off with a groan. 'Oh well, 'ow was I ter know? It looked all right to me, and I went upstairs. Begin at the top and work your way down, is my motto. Well, I hadn't half begun when I heard a car draw up and stop. I nearly threw a ruddy fit. And before I could think which way to run, the front door opened and someone came in. I stood at the top of the stairs fairly holding me breath, I can tell you. And then, blimey, if another car didn't race up and stop. I heard the bell ring and ring, and a ruddy little dog bark, and me heart was in me mouth. Then I heard someone start coming up them stairs, and I slipped back and stood behind the bathroom door out of sight. They was dragging something that went bump, bump, bump on the stairs. They opened first one door . . . then another . . . then they went downstairs again and let in the bloke who was still hammering on the front door. I heard 'em talking.

'Looked like I'd made a mistake thinking the house was empty, didn't it? More like a house-party, it was turning out to be. And me stuck up there, not knowing whether to wait for them to leave or to chance me arm and go first.

'I got sick of it in the end. The bathroom window was only a foot square, I couldn't get out that way, so I moved as quietly as I could into one of the other rooms. I opened the door soft and I closed it soft behind me. I could just hear their voices coming up faintly through the floor. It was dark as hell. I slid forward a bit and stuck out my hand to feel the way, so that I didn't knock into anything.

'I touched something dampish and soft and ran my hand over something oddly shaped with bumps, and then on to hair or fur . . . no, hair . . . ' Slimy licked his lips and swallowed. 'It was sort of uncanny, I couldn't make out what it was, and yet I felt I ought to reckernise it, and I didn't half like the feel, either. So I flashed a glim . . . Christ! What do you think it was? A woman! Lying on her back with her mouth open, like she was snoring. Only she wasn't snoring. And I'd gorn and stuck my hand on her face. Pushed me fingers right in her bleeding mouth. And rubbed me hand clean over her nose and eyes and hair. And I hadn't woke her up. Sleeping like the dead she was.'

He munched his fingers in silence for a moment, re-living the horror of that moment.

'Yes, she was dead, all right. Couldn't make any mistake about that, even though I'd never seen a corpse before. I wasn't in the war,' he added apologetically. 'Oooh! It didn't half turn me up, I can promise you. And then I thought, well, what's she doing on the floor, and not in the bed? And why has she got all her clothes on still? People didn't ought to die in their boots, as the saying is, did they? And then I remembered that horrid bumping noise I'd heard on the stairs . . . And I didn't like it, see, I didn't like it at all. And I thought, Jesus, I'd better get the hell out of here before anything worse happens. For I thought, if there had been any funny business, and I got mixed up in it in any way . . . So I did a running bunk and knocked something clean over with a bloody awful crash. Gawd, I was scared! I expected any minute that one of the blokes down below would come up to see what happened. And the noise my heart made was like a ruddy dynamo, I thought it was going to give out on me. And then, as soon as I dared move, I got the window open. The sash went up easy, and that was the only bit of luck I had that night. Then I got out, and I didn't stop to say good-bye to anyone, you can take my word for it. I didn't stop moving till I got to Poinings. And that's all I know about it, so help me Gawd!' he concluded piously.

'You'd have done better to go to the police with your story straight away,' was the inspector's comment.

'I didn't know anything, did I, sir? Nice dummy I should have looked if I'd gone and narked all about it and then we'd found the lady had died natural. Never trouble trouble till trouble troubles you, I say. It's bad enough now.'

'It is indeed.'

'I never laid a finger on her, I swear.'

'Someone did. If they don't escape us it's no thanks to you. You didn't see either of the two people downstairs, either then or at some other time?'

Slimy shook his head.

'You never looked through the hinge in the bathroom door to see who it was coming up the stairs, bumpety-bump?'

'It was dark,' he said simply.

'And the dead woman, what was she like?'

Slimy shuddered.

'She was very small and thin. Her face was sort of twisted up and only the whites of her eyes showed. Her hair was dark.'

'All right. That'll do for now. Go and wait over there till they've typed out your statement for you to sign.'

And in the fullness of time, the

statement was typed, read through, and signed by Slimy Joe, and dispatched to the St. John's Wood Police Station, where it lay on top of the three-quarters full dossier to await Inspector Johnson's design.

Inspector Johnson, by a piece of typical ill-fortune that attends us all from time to time, was called away to attend the Shropshire Assizes, where he was witness in an important case. He was away a week altogether and he did not receive Phoebe's card until he came back.

It was the first time he had seen her handwriting, and he stared at its cryptic message with a smile that only the kind-hearted would not call fatuous. He read it several times for pleasure, without taking in its meaning.

It read:

'Is it fish, fowl, or good red herring?'
P.M. 32 Abbey Mansions.

As soon as he came off duty he rang her up, ostensibly to learn the meaning of her latest quip. He tried three times at intervals of half-an-hour, but got no reply. Then he rang through to the porter, who informed him casually that Mrs. Moore had gone away, he was not sure for how long, but she had been gone about a week already, he thought.

Inspector Johnson put down the receiver slowly. Only then did he ask himself the significance of the quotation. His frowning brow crumpled with anxiety, like a bloodhound's, as he tried to elucidate the absurd prankish message which was plainly meant to be a clue. She was so childishly impulsive!

She must mean she was on the track of something — something of course to do with her sister's murder. He seemed to hear her saying in her light teasing voice: 'Doesn't it seem fishy? Is it something foul? Or is it, after all, just another red herring?' He banged the desk savagely with his fist in a kind of anguish at the thought of her folly, at the realization that the card was already a week old. *A week old!* Christ! He must hurry, hurry, hurry! He must not think he might be too late.

5

The Kill

Against the slate-coloured hill, covered here and there in coarse bleached grass spangled with sea-pink and bold dandelions, there stood out very plain and square a small white bungalow, overlooking the sea. A rough road led steeply past it, from the village at the bottom to the scattered and impermanent bungalow community spreading across the hilltop to the sea. And in between the two lay this little summer house, as light and fragile as an eggshell, in which dwelt the two women who had unconsciously entered the field of the eternal conflict, and from which one or other must emerge the victor.

Miss Lowell never left her for long at a time, so Phoebe had little opportunity to pry among the hidden papers or open locked drawers. Not that Miss Lowell was fool enough to keep anything incriminating. Nor had she the kind of criminal vanity that keeps a scrapbook of newspaper cuttings relating to her crimes. Her vanity was sweet and secret, she never felt the impulse to communicate her diabolical cleverness to other people, for long years ago she had learnt how to be entirely-self-contained. She despised people. Why should she wish to tell them of her deeds?

Her problem at the moment was to persuade Mrs. Abrams that her health was not all it should be, that she should consult a doctor about this 'tropical heart.' Mrs. Abrams maintained that she was now much better and that her heart no longer bothered her. If she had occasion to go to London she would see a Harley Street specialist, she promised.

Miss Lowell longed for the sexual fascination of George Joseph Smith, who had carted his infatuated women off to the doctor's consulting-room with the greatest of ease; but then it was only natural for a loving husband to be anxious for his spouse's health, and it was considered a pretty thought. Miss Lowell perforce lacked that particular art. She relied instead on gentle persuasion. She pointed out that it was mainly selfishness on her part to wish Mrs. Abrams to have the benefit of a doctor, but while she was staying with her it was rather a burden of responsibility; should anything untoward occur it would not look well for Miss Lowell. Of course that was being pessimistic and envisaging the remotest possibilities, such an eventuality was unlikely, but one should prepare the path and not shirk one's minor duties because they were boring or unpleasant, etc., etc. Put like that, there was little Mrs. Abrams could do but give in.

She went down to Falmouth to visit a doctor there who had been recommended to her. What passed between them remained confidential, but when Mrs. Abrams returned she looked distressed, her pale face paler than ever, her sparkling aquamarine eyes dulled and introspective. From time to time she pressed her hand nervously to her heart. She admitted over supper that night that the doctor had not given a good report of her: she must take care of herself, rest more, not get excited, not be energetic — or he would not answer for the consequences.

That was all Miss Lowell needed to know, as Phoebe was aware. Phoebe was genuinely afraid, she hated the job she had voluntarily undertaken, never knowing from what quarter the blow, when it came, would fall. Was she to be edged over the cliff? Was she to be gassed or drowned in the bath? Was she to be poisoned, as poor Florence was? And if so, how was she to be induced to take it?

Every meal became a torment of suspicion. She watched Miss Lowell incessantly for some betraying factor. Every hour there increased her danger, brought her potential doom that much nearer. For she had no doubt — since she had deliberately proffered herself as a victim — that Miss Lowell intended to kill her. The only snag was which of them would attain their objective first. Would Miss Lowell succeed in killing her before she had acquired the positive proof she

340

was risking her life to get?

They were enjoying a spell of fine weather and in the afternoon Miss Lowell pottered happily about the tiny garden, still as crude to look at in its own way as the bungalow; or knelt devoutly hour upon hour, weeding the herbaceous border; while Mrs. Abrams reclined languidly in a deck chair, her arms dangling at her side, her face upturned to the sun, sleeping perhaps, or thinking her own deep thoughts. Sometimes she would open her eyes suddenly to find Miss Lowell standing beside her with her head on one side and a benign expression on her face, like a cat that has been at the cream; then Mrs. Abrams would blink drowsily and smile back, but the inner shiver that she felt at such moments left her feeling cold for hours afterwards despite the warmth of the sun. She contrived to escape from her gentle jailor for long enough to make some small purchases at the chemist's not far away, and, charming the white-coated gentleman behind the counter, persuaded him to let her use the telephone in his little back room. It took but a few precious minutes to make arrangements with the Falmouth police. She felt better when that was done. Now it was too late to draw back, she would have to go through with it.

She was keyed up, sick with excitement and apprehension as if it were a First Night, as she changed that evening into a simple black dinner dress — black, because she was in mourning of course — and with a determination that was belied by her trembling fingers, she fastened at the neck of her frock the little miniature brooch which had belonged to her sister.

In the living-room the folding gate-legged table was laid for the evening meal, and Miss Lowell was still in the kitchenette. She could be heard humming tunelessly to herself. Phoebe sat down directly beneath the light, facing the doorway, waiting to see Miss Lowell's expression when she entered. So much depended on it.

But Miss Lowell when she came in glanced at Mrs. Abrams with her customary red-faced benevolence. She was surprisingly unobservant of details of dress and such-like matters. Her head at that moment was full of more important thoughts. While Miss Lowell was engrossed in petting her little dog, Belinda, and feeding her with scraps from her own plate, and talking to her in the peculiar baby-whine she reserved for her, Phoebe loosened the fastening of her brooch, so that in a few moments it would slide out of the thin material. It fell with a little tinkle.

'Oh!' exclaimed Mrs. Abrams on a high-pitched note. And her hand flew to the neck of her dress: 'My brooch!' Beneath the table her toe pushed it nearer to Miss Lowell. 'I ought not to wear it; the fastening is insecure: it's always coming undone. Can you see it? I think it went on the floor.'

Miss Lowell picked it up and turned it over curiously, her face expressionless and flushed — perhaps from stooping.

'You are admiring it?' said Mrs. Abrams. 'It is pretty, isn't it? And unusual, too: you won't see another like it. I'm very fond of it; that's why I wear it so often. But I must get the catch seen to.'

'Very,' said Miss Lowell in a flat voice, stretching her lips into the semblance of a smile. 'Where did you find it?'

'Give! Give!' said Mrs. Abrams playfully, holding out her hand palm upwards.

Miss Lowell returned it to its owner with something akin to reluctance. 'Where did I find it? It's been in the family for years, my dear. It belonged to my sister.'

'Your sister? I didn't know ... I thought ... ' stammered Miss Lowell. 'You told me you had no relatives.'

Leah Abrams laughed and shook her red hair back from her shoulders. 'Oh, come! I can't believe I really said that. I must have had a mother and father at some time or other or I wouldn't be here, would I? I must have said I have no relatives living, and that is the sad truth. The family is rapidly dying out: when I am gone ... And I am not likely to last much longer, am I? We are none of us long-lived. My sister was not forty, poor darling, when she ... ' Leah Abrams broke off, as her lips trembled and her eyes filled with tears. She dabbed at them discreetly with a handkerchief.

Phoebe's heart was thumping evenly but painfully so that it was an effort to breathe naturally. 'Let us talk of something more cheerful,' she said.

But a strained silence succeeded. There seemed nothing to say.

Miss Lowell stroked the Cairn's small bony skull remorselessly, absently, while her thoughts ran feverishly along one corridor after another in search of an escape.

Leah Abrams was preoccupied in refastening her brooch into her frock. At last she said meditatively:

'As a matter of fact I came across it quite by chance in a little shop off Lamb's Conduit Street. It was something of a blow to me, you can imagine. I bought it because I was reluctant to let it go out of the family . . . and because . . . because I thought it would be a useful bit of evidence.'

Miss Lowell said: 'Don't you like your supper? You aren't eating a thing. Can I get you something else? An egg?'

'Thank you. I'm not hungry.' There was again a few moments uncomfortable pause, and then Phoebe said mockingly: 'I'm disappointed in you, Miss Lowell. I made sure you would say, 'Evidence for what?''

Miss Lowell looked at her blankly.

'It is a mistake to take things for granted, isn't it? Why should you think I would ask that?'

'I thought your curiosity would be greater than your fear.'

Miss Lowell stacked the plates into a neat pile. She said frankly: 'Do you know, Mrs. Abrams, I think we are talking about different things suddenly. I no longer follow you.'

'I think you follow me very well, on the contrary.'

Miss Lowell laughed pleasantly and stood up with an armful of plates.

'Shall we postpone this conversation to some other time, then? We seem to be rather at cross-purposes just now.'

'This is not a business to be postponed. Please sit down, Miss Lowell — or Mrs. Jolly, or whatever your name is.'

Miss Lowell sat down again quietly and put the stack of plates back on to the table.

'You see,' said Mrs. Abrams agreeably, 'after all there is something to be discussed.'

'Well?' said Miss Lowell, her honest kindly eyes suddenly as hard as steel.

'I've been looking for you a long time, and it is a strange relief to have met you as last. You know who I am now, don't you? I'm Florence Brown's sister.'

'She never — ' cried Miss Lowell involuntarily, and then closed her mouth like a trap.

'Ah, but she had! She may never have mentioned me because she had quarrelled with me, but I was there in the background all the time. Only I was not able to save her. But that is not going to help you, Miss Lowell, or Mrs. Jolly.' She leant forward with narrowed eyes: 'Or is your name Violet Russell?' she asked distinctly, and laughed at the woman's expression. 'Ah ha, you thought I could know nothing really! You thought I was bluffing, and that if you sat tight and kept your mouth shut you would be all right. You fool! Hasn't it dawned on you yet that this time *you* are the victim? I baited the trap with myself as decoy and you walked in. Now it's clanged shut behind you and you'll never get out again.' Phoebe's lips curved cruelly and her eyes glittered.

Miss Lowell rose slowly from her chair, as one stunned with horror.

'I think you must be mad!' she exclaimed in slow accents, her eyes round with terror. 'I've never heard anyone in my life before . . . I don't understand one word . . . I don't know a Florence Brown. So far as I remember I've never met such a person. I can only conclude that you are a lunatic . . . I'm not staying another moment in the house with you alone.' As she spoke she was backing gradually to the door, keeping the chair always before her.

Almost in one movement Phoebe pushed the table to one side and leapt from her chair in a stride that carried her halfway across the room with a velocity that caused her to slide the rest of the way and land with a crash against the door, her arms outstretched defensively. 'Oh, no, you don't!' she gasped.

Miss Lowell swung her head this way and that.

'How dare you! Let me by at once!'

Their eyes met, full of defiance and terror, in an attempt to outstare the other. It was as though time stood still and had locked the two women in these frozen attitudes forever. Neither dared break the spell.

Phoebe thought, this is absurd. We can't stand staring at one another for ever. I shall lose my advantage if I don't do something soon.

But already she was too late. Without warning, Miss Lowell raised the chair vertically above her head and smashed it down with all her force where Phoebe stood.

But in the endless second of its descending Phoebe had time to fling herself sideways so that she caught the edge of the blow on the point of her shoulder.

Even that made her stagger and slip

and fall on one knee. If she had received it in its entirety it would have knocked her senseless. The force of it broke the chair and splintered a panel of the door.

Belinda rushed forth from where she had been crouching beneath the table, yapping excitedly, and hurled herself at Phoebe's slender ankles, and attempted to bury her sharp pointed teeth therein. Phoebe kicked her brutally, catching the little bitch in her soft belly with the tip of her shoe and sending her yelping through the air.

Miss Lowell went quite livid. Her mouth fell open in a rictus that was a kind of savage smile. Phoebe instinctively put up her hands to protect her face. She thought desperately, what am I supposed to do? Why did I ever get myself into this mess? Moving steadily backwards away from Miss Lowell, she was brought up suddenly with the wall behind her.

'This won't do you any good,' said Phoebe.

Miss Lowell's fist smashed into her mouth. She glanced in an instant's surprise at her bleeding knuckles.

'Nor you, either,' she rejoined exultantly. Never before had she been able to touch anyone, to hurt anyone deliberately, or even to watch anyone suffer. Now she was released from that inhibition. It gave her an almost sexual satisfaction to batter her fists into Phoebe's soft white face, to hear her gasp.

But not so satisfying when Phoebe's hand was at her throat, pressing her back, pressing in her windpipe so that it was an agony, pressing with full vigour the carotid arteries so that the blood throbbed in her head and a mist streaked with sharp lights was before her eyes. Her own fingers plucked weakly at the other's hand . . . It was getting dark . . .

Phoebe watching her anxiously, terrified that she would let go too soon, terrified equally that she would hold on too long and kill her, saw her eyes bolting from their sockets and her face empurple alarmingly, and suddenly loosened her hold. Miss Lowell fell on to the floor and lay there moaning, a hand at her throat.

Phoebe swayed backwards and forwards uncertainly . . . aware of an immense exhaustion which threatened to overwhelm her.

She must have been mad, she acknowledged. They were probably both of them insane, when she considered how they had just been behaving. Rolling round the room, fighting. Two middle-aged women-of-the-world fighting like a couple of whores in a cat-house. It was incredible! It was obscene! It was laughable!

And she would have laughed if her split and swollen lip had not prevented her. Her head ached intolerably and her face was stiff and throbbing all over. She patted tenderly at the blood still running down from a cut beneath one eye. She must look a horrid sight. Her head was sore where Miss Lowell had tugged out a handful of bright hair. She glanced down at the woman. What was she to do with her? She ought she supposed vaguely to tie her up. But with what?

Belinda was licking her mistress's face. Miss Lowell sat up, her white hair dishevelled, her face deadly pale, the eyes ringed ominously. Phoebe wondered which of them was the worse wreck.

'Help me up, please.' Miss Lowell spoke without looking at her, in a hoarse croak. She stood there, hanging on to the mantelpiece with one hand and her head with the other. 'I don't know what came over me . . . ' she muttered with difficulty. 'When you kicked my doggy . . . I saw red.'

Phoebe forbore to point out that she had opened the attack before that by attempting to brain her with the chair,

'Before we go any further, I must have something to take — or I shall — my throat . . . ' complained the older woman. 'Will you allow me to get you something? I need a really good cup of tea myself, I don't know about you.'

Phoebe intimated that it would not be unwelcome. She sat there quietly, busy with her thoughts, half-listening to the sounds in the kitchen, secure in the knowledge that Miss Lowell could not get away without being seen by her.

Miss Lowell brought in two cups of tea on a tray. Phoebe took hers without a word, still lost in thought, and walked over to the window. She stirred it mechanically once or twice and then raised it to her lips . . . Suddenly she gave a loud cry and the cup crashed on the floor, spattering her feet with hot tea. But Miss Lowell did not turn, she stared before her unperturbed with a look of smug satisfaction. She did not turn when she heard the breath rattle with a hideous whining sound in Leah Abrams' throat; she did not turn even when she heard her fall heavily to the ground, nor yet when her heels grated spasmodically once or twice against the polished boards. Only when silence had prolonged itself a little way into the room did Miss Lowell turn to survey her victim.

Leah Abrams was not a pretty picture lying there awkwardly with her battered face half-turned to the light, but Miss Lowell seemed to find some sweet satisfaction in it, to judge from the pleased expression on her face. Miss Lowell kicked her venomously. 'That's for Belinda,' she said. 'And that's for me.'

The bell rang piercingly, more agonizingly than conscience. Miss Lowell went stiff as a corpse. The bell rang again. The blood beat heavily back into her face. She had been through all this before in some other life, in some dream, she thought dimly, and struggled to her feet, her lips moving in inaudible and ceaseless prayer. She seized Phoebe by her heels and dragged her ruthlessly into the bedroom, banging her against the door-posts in her haste. A minute before she was rejoicing in the death of her enemy. Now she would have given ten years of her life for her to be still living. She rolled her under the bed and pulled the counter pane low so that it touched the carpet.

While she was out of the room, a hand pushed through the splintered panel of the front door and, groping downward, found and turned the handle. The bell rang again.

Miss Lowell returned. Started to pick up the broken teacup and —

'Oh no, you don't,' said a voice in her ear. A hand caught her wrist. A hand carefully relieved her of the encumbering fragments. 'Thank you so much. We shall need those. Important evidence, you know.'

She screamed horribly, her face distorted with inhuman terror. Somehow she wrenched her arm free and with a wild lunge reached the door and freedom . . . running madly into the night towards the cliff top . . .

'Not that way,' said Inspector Johnson. 'You don't deserve it.' And the air was shrill and vibrant with police whistles and running feet . . . The little black dog stood in the doorway and howled hideously, and then pattered slowly into the dark wilderness.

Inspector Johnson stood there a moment feeling leaden-sick with apprehension before moving like a stone towards the door through which Phoebe had been dragged. He tried to keep his mind deliberately numb and murmured lines of poetry to starve off thought, till he found himself saying, 'dear dead woman, with such hair too,' and felt a searing anguish stab his heart, his throat, his eyes . . .

And then incredibly he saw her sitting there before the dressing-table, dabbing her bruised face with skin lotion. He stared at her open-mouthed. He nearly said aloud, Thank God you're alive! And then all his conflicting emotions resolved surprisingly into a surge of fury. He wanted to shake her for having frightened him so, as a mother slaps her child for being nearly run over.

She jumped nervously when she saw his reflection in the dusky depths of the mirror, but she did not turn round. She smiled at him coolly enough and went on patting tenderly at her wounds, waiting to hear his fair words of praise for her pluck and guile, waiting for the chance to graciously forgive his blunderings.

She was the more taken aback when he said in an edged voice: 'Well, I hope you're pleased with yourself.'

'I am rather,' she said lightly.

His voice was stern with disapproval. 'You had no right to go off like that. You might have been killed.'

She said airily: 'Oh, I knew you'd step in at the psychological moment like a storybook hero.'

He felt himself flush heavily with the suppression of inward rage. 'Indeed! It may interest you to know that I was away and didn't return till yesterday. And if I had not chanced to return then I should not have got your message and you would probably be dead by now.'

She said spitefully, trying to hide the shaking of her lower lip: 'I suppose you think you saved my life by grimacing at me outside the window and nearly frightening me out of my wits! It's only because I'm such a consummate actress that I was able to turn it to my own advantage. Do you imagine I didn't *know* she was going to try and poison me? I deliberately gave her the opportunity, so as to get the final proof I wanted. But you nearly ruined it all by butting in too soon. Isn't that typical of the police! They ruin everything.'

'Thank you so much,' he said haughtily. 'Doubtless you would have managed better without me. I won't intrude any longer.'

'Come back,' she called frantically, sinking her hurt pride instantly of necessity. 'Don't leave me alone here, for God's sake. Thoughtless, selfish beast,' she muttered to herself, almost in tears from the strain and shock of the last few hours.

'Yes, I am,' he admitted, shamefaced. 'Forgive me! I don't know what came over me. You gave me such a terrible scare. I thought you were dead.'

'What!' she exclaimed delightedly. 'You really did? I fooled you too? You see, I am a good actress, aren't I? I told you I was. Were you really frightened?'

'It was worse than fright,' he growled unhappily. 'The bottom had dropped out of the world. That was why, when I walked in here and saw you calmly sitting there fixing your face, I felt suddenly absolutely mad with you. And so I was rude and angry, like a mother slapping her child because it wasn't run over after all.'

They gazed at one another in silence in the mirror.

'I *was* glad to see you,' she said softly at last. 'But never frighten me like that again as long as I live.'

'So long as we live together,' he amended, and took her gently in his arms.

Other titles in the
Linford Mystery Library:

DEATH DIMENSION

Denis Hughes

When airline pilot Robert Varden's plane is wrecked in a thunderstorm, he goes to bail out. As he claws his way through the escape hatch, he is struck by lightning and his consciousness fades into oblivion. Miraculously, Varden cheats death, and awakes in hospital after doctors succeed in saving his life. But he emerges into an unfamiliar world that is on the brink of devastating war, and where his friends are mysteriously seventeen years older than he remembered them . . .

MRS. WATSON AND THE DEATH CULT

Michael Mallory

When the body of a prominent businessman is found floating in an ancient Roman bath, all the evidence points to a young man named Ronald Standish as the murderer. His wife appeals to her old governess Amelia, the second wife of Dr. John H. Watson, for help. Soon, Amelia is thrust into a baffling mystery involving the practice of ancient pagan religious rites in the modern city of Bath. At every step, though, she finds evidence that makes the case against Standish even stronger . . .